# The Tammersford Lot

By

Rosie Driffill

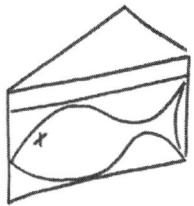

*Fishcake Publications*

# The Tammersford Lot

Published by Fishcakes Publications

Huddersfield

www.fishcakepublications.com

ISBN 978-1-909015-43-2

Paperback Edition

© **Rosie Driffill 2016.**

All Rights Reserved.

First Edition Published in Great Britain in 2016.

Cover Photography by Rosie Driffill

Title, character and place names are all protected by the applicable laws. This book is a work of fiction, therefore names, characters and events are fictitious and any resemblance to an actual person, living or dead, or any actual event is purely coincidental.

All rights reserved. No part of this publication may be reproduced, stored in a retrieval system or transmitted in any form or by any means, electronic, mechanical, photocopying, recording or otherwise, without prior permission from copyright owners.

## About the Author

Rosie is a freelance journalist based in the north of England. She has written for the Dalesman, Wanderlust and the Huffington Post, and contributes a monthly piece to the Guardian's Mind Your Language blog. A huge language enthusiast, Rosie is also at the helm of a new enterprise for promoting language teaching and learning, a feat which complements her creative writing to the degree that she wants readers to think about how far language can really convey what we mean it to.

The Tammersford Lot is Rosie's first collection of short stories. She also writes poetry and dabbles in illustration, as well as penning comic pieces that satirise the human world under the guide of an ex-penguin (see http://www.expenguin.com).

## Contents

A Window Seat ................................................................................. 1

Miss Lee on the Moorland ............................................................... 8

Dress Lady ...................................................................................... 16

Clara's Home Job ........................................................................... 19

Young Codgers ............................................................................... 22

Before the Shopping Trip ............................................................... 27

Good People ................................................................................... 32

Mrs Boden ...................................................................................... 37

Bottles ............................................................................................. 45

Selena and Edward ......................................................................... 48

The Rowan Tree ............................................................................. 55

Anne Moon ..................................................................................... 78

## A Window Seat

Greg realised he must have been reading for a while, because when he looked out of the window, he noticed that the train had ceased to cut against the grain of the land. From what he could make out through the afternoon drizzle, the ground had become coarse and uneven; brown, white, and bumpy, like a bucket of conches, and the sky – no longer blue, but newspaper grey and backlit by an ailing sun – was caught behind a fretwork of bare trees.

Seeing that his son had arisen from his text, Frank Moon placed a hemming pin on the table. As the train rounded a bend in the track, the pin rocked on its orange tip. It reminded Greg of a tiny arum stalk nudged by a breeze.

Frank said, 'Just had that go right through my finger.' He looked at Greg, then directed a forensic glare at his wife.

'Look, it didn't go right through your finger and I've already said I was sorry!' His wife was fixing her hair in her pocket mirror. 'Oh, I can't see a thing in this. Here, I'm just going to nip to the toilet and try sort this crow's nest out. Do you think I should have it up, or do you think it'll look better down, but with the front bits pinned back?'

'Up. And you can get me a few more tissues and bin this while you're there.' Frank handed her a scrunched serviette.

'Don't be so daft, it was only a scratch. Look!' She spread the serviette on the table. Greg noticed a small, red blotch in its centre. 'I don't think you'll be quite needing a blood transfusion, dear!'

'Yes, well, you're lucky I'm not a haemophiliac, that's all I can say!'

'Hypochondriac, more like. Shift, will you? We'll be there soon and I look like the Wreck of the Hesperus.' She called back as she left, '*No you don't darling, you look beautiful, as always!*'

## The Tammersford Lot

Sashaying her way down the carriage, Greg wouldn't have called his mother beautiful, exactly, but certainly attractive. She had a long back, like a Scandinavian type, which rendered her tall, important looking, and required that the rest of her frame be slightly larger than that which might merit an association with beauty. Handsome, you might have said, though considering her strict morning ablutions and unremitting attention to her appearance, such a term may have jarred with her more feminine sense of self.

The carriage was brightly lit and crowded, and with the windows shut and the heating on, the air was musty on account of peoples' damp clothes. Frank made sure his wife had passed through the far doors, before turning back to Greg.

'I tell you what, though, son,' his tone was matter-of-fact, 'I must be a tough old sod. Impaled me, that thing did, but I managed to contain myself.' He inspected his fat finger and made to place it between his lips, before thinking better of it. 'Bloody impaled me.'

'What were you doing with it?'

'Me? Nothing! What would I want with a bloody sewing pin? It's your mother's. She was using it to fix that rose to her hat. I just reached up to adjust it because it looked like it was about to fall out, and I went and bloody ... stabbed myself! Knocked the rose clean off the hat. Now the hat's in her bag and the flower's in the bin.'

'Why did you put it in the bin?'

'I don't know. A few petals fell off so it looks uneven, apparently.'

'Can't she just wear the hat without the rose?'

'No idea. It's too drab, or something.'

'Here, pass me the flower.'

'What, from the bin?'

'Yes.'

'Why?'

'I just want to see the damage.'

'Ah, get off with you, soft lad, you don't want to go bothering with that. Here, get a load of this instead...' Frank glanced behind him, dug into his blazer pocket and pulled out a hip flask. It was silver, with a mottled finish. 'Go on, have some. Go on, before she gets back.'

'I'm alright. I want to keep a clear head until after my reading.'

'Here, what son doesn't accept a free drink off his old dad?' Frank cocked his head back and shook half the contents into his mouth, his eyes – small and black as moles – blinking rapidly. 'Bloody reading. I'm sure they'll be well capable of living happily ever after once they're married without your input. Why make such a flipping fuss over-'

'Mum's coming.'

He screwed the lid back on in haste and stuffed it back in his blazer. He said to his wife, 'You went with the down 'do in the end, then?'

'Yes, but I'm not convinced by it.' She handed him a wad of tissues. 'Got this magazine that might give me a few ideas, though.' Dropping her find on the table, she proceeded to browse through it. 'How's the war wound?'

'It's still bleeding, look! Here, you wouldn't lick it for me, would you?'

'Why ever would I want to do that?'

'Well, it's an open wound what needs washing, doesn't it? And I can't stand the taste of blood, me.'

'Well, neither can I! Go and run it under the cold tap.'

'No way. Hey, you know where they get their water supply, don't you, these trains?'

'No, enlighten me.' She licked her own finger and turned the page.

'Bloody recycle it from the toilets, don't they? I'm not having that garbage getting into my system.'

'Here, do you think I should do my hair like hers?' Mrs Moon held a page up to the light. 'See how she's scooped the top bits back but left the rest down? I mean, I know hers is a bit

*3*

straighter than mine but if I brushed it through, I reckon it'd look pretty similar. Hasn't she got a strange face, though? Hey, I bet if she only had a few minutes to sort her hair out she'd still look a real fright.'

'Well, Jane Drew will have done hers like that, won't she?' Frank replied replacing one tissue with another. 'This won't let up, you know. And don't even get me started on the pain.'

'Hey, that's a point. Hey, I never thought of that. And she needn't bother tying hers up 'cause she only just recently had it layered, didn't she?'

'Well I don't know why you're asking me - reckon I'm going to bleed to death before I clap eyes on Jane's barnet!'

'Do you know, I think I will put the top bits up, just to spite her. I swear that woman's always trying to approach on my territory. I told her on the phone I was wearing duck egg blue – duck egg blue – and I wouldn't be surprised if she turned up all kitted out in it as well.'

'Well, her bloody husband's just as bad. Can't stand anyone doing better than him, can he? If you've got two bathrooms, he's got four, with a Jacuzzi in three of them and a nineteen-year old mermaid in the other. Hey, and don't forget to tell him you're working for me now, lad. That should shut him up – in fact he oughtn't start bragging 'cause he's been out of work since they scrapped all them bus routes. And his son might be getting put away, nasty piece of work that he is.'

Greg shifted in his seat. Slowly, he ran his finger over four conical protrusions in the table's paintwork. Frank's wife looked up, first at Frank, then at Greg. But she said nothing.

'You want me to tell Mr Drew I'm working for you, or that you're training me?' Greg kept his eyes on the table. 'Because technically, I'm not working for you yet, am I?'

'Never mind that, lad, he's not to know. Just make sure that if he asks you, you know what an architrave is.'

'Why?'

'Well, because he knows his stuff. I mean, we used to work together, didn't we, him and I? And that son of his, for a time.

So I'll look like a right daft sod if you get it wrong! No good saying you're working for me and not knowing what a flaming architrave is.'

'So just to confirm, I'm to tell people I work for you?'

'Not people, just him. And if he does ask you something and you don't know the answer, just say "well, that's my dad's area really." Or, "my old man specialises in that." And then tell him you specialise in architraves.'

'And if he asks me about the last thing I did with an architrave?'

'Well I don't know, lad, improvise! Tell him you wrote a bloody poem about it.' He pointed his finger at Greg, momentarily letting the tissue hang loose. 'Don't you dare, mind.'

'Have you practised your reading, dear?' Mrs Moon asked from behind her magazine.

'It's only twelve lines,' said Greg. He rubbed his eyes. 'I may change the last line to "Shall happiness bloom."'

'What was it before, again?' Mrs Moon brought the magazine up to her nose, then held it at length, scrunching and relaxing her face as her eyes adjusted. 'Do you know, I can't make out who that is she's with. He's playing with her ear lobe, look!'

'It was "Shall happiness reign." There aren't any other regal metaphors in the poem, though. On the other hand, I've mentioned flowers twice.'

'I'm sure they'll love it.'

'I'm sure they'll be wondering why there aren't any other bloody regal metaphors in it.' Frank sucked a laugh over his teeth. He was down to his final tissue. 'Here, love, hold that on for me, will you? I'm going to ruin the other hand with repetitive strain.'

'Go and run,' his wife replied. 'Right, I'm going to settle for that one, the one with the side ponytail. I like the way she's swept it over – gives it more volume. Although...although do you think I should pin it up? I think I'll just pin it up.' She

## The Tammersford Lot

paused for a moment to think, her top lip clamped tightly over its lower counterpart and drawn into a sharp point. She looked like an irritated owl, big eyes too, the works. Her fringe was level in length, but varied in colour, and spaced unevenly across her forehead. What should have been one facial feature was in fact – by way of an unfortunate sequence of calf licks – three; a head of blonde and grey wire assembled by nature into a crude triptych.

'Look, just bloody get on with it, will you, we'll be there any minute!' Frank ordered. 'There we are, that woodland bit in the distance – where the trees come together in a triangle, down the hill. There's Mason's Forest. And Tammersford is just at the bottom, so get your stuff together because I imagine we'll be pulling in in about three minutes.'

'Right, let me just dash to the toilet to sort my hair one last time,' said Mrs Moon. She gestured for Frank to stand up and let her pass. 'God knows what I'm going to do with it - it'll just have to be a panic job.'

Outside, the scene was still. A bright, wintery light exploded over the unruptured crust of a frozen lake, and the trees remained as constant in their reflection as in themselves. Greg had always supposed that people gazing intently out of train windows were really just inspecting their own image, so took care to ensure that each glance was nothing more than fleeting.

He straightened his blazer. 'In poetry, I feel like…well I feel quite like I'm being as honest as any man can be. You'll find more falsehoods in those magazines and in conversation with Mr Drew than you will in any poem. If it's all the same to you, I'd rather be honest with him, if he asks me anything, that is.'

Leaning forward across the table Frank pointed at Greg. 'Listen you, don't go round telling everyone you're a bloody poet,' he said. The tissue held only for a moment upon his outstretched finger before falling to the floor.

'I write poetry. I didn't say I was a poet.'

'It's a lost cause, I keep telling you. No one wants to listen to a bloke twittering on about floral metaphors. And you will tell Jane's husband you're working for me...' Frank took a final swig from his hipflask, '...and do it with a bloody smile on your face. By, if I met a bloke your age with a face as long as yours, I'd tell him to wait 'til he had kids. Then he'd have something to whine about.' He held the flask out to Greg.

'Really, I'm fine,' Greg replied.

'You'll share a beer with your old dad later though, won't you?'

'You've stopped bleeding, by the looks of things.'

'I mean, you'll be wanting a beer later, won't you?'

'The best thing you can do now is elevate your hand.'

Frank was looking at Greg directly. He had begun tapping his fingers on the tabletop, slowly at first, then rapidly, palm down and all. 'Surely you'll have a drink with your old dad later, though?'

Greg's eyes met his father's before tracking the view once more. Outside, the drizzle had subsided, leaving an assault of grey and white tines across the sky. The train began to slow. Greg tested the words reign and bloom against one another, breathing each syllable onto the window until the glass was impastoed with a cloud of white breath. Eventually he asked, 'What would you do if that pin went through your finger again?'

'Well, I'm a tough old sod, me. I could take it.' Frank Moon retrieved the tissue and held it around his finger. As his fingers tightened, so did his lips. 'And if anyone asks, I was tough in the bloody first place. Tell them I was tough in the first place. Tell them we laughed about it. Tell them I barely mentioned it.'

## Miss Lee on the Moorland

My train finally pulled into Tammersford, and I expected there to be a crowd in the Tap and Snake. Instead, after an eight-hour journey, the station master told me that it had been closed for several months. I said I had a lot of loose change to spend and was very disappointed to hear that; he said the council had agreed it was no longer fit for purpose.

I lingered on the platform. An old man in a grey suit told me I'd get along in the Boar's Head, but he let me walk almost to the gate before calling me back. He said he was sorry, son, but he didn't mean the Boar's Head; he meant the Cockerel. He still called it by its old name because you just can't teach an old boar new tricks, ha ha ha. He had a long blazer and short legs; his clothes and his skin seemed stale, matted.

Finding the pub wasn't difficult. I kept the tip of the moorland in my line of sight, as the old man had advised me to do, because losing it would have meant I'd dipped too low into the town and the great thing about the Cockerel was that it stayed well out of all that. I wondered, all what? Tammersford would always do. You had all your basic needs met, in the town, and as soon as you wanted out, there were days of countryside to get lost in. That's what my father used to say.

I could tell by the pub's rotting brickwork and the fold belt of turned, humped male backs that 'great' was purely in the eye of the beholder. I liked to think that after the year I'd had, a reticent clientele wouldn't bother me, but I didn't take more than one drink, and as soon as I'd made up my mind to book a room (I had to stay somewhere), I went promptly upstairs. The landlord told me I wasn't to come in any later than midnight and that he'd have to take three separate deposits from me: one for the room key, one for the towels and one for remote. I wanted to ask him why he needed a deposit for the remote and not for the television, but then I caught sight of myself in a brass kettle and saw the small, facial groove I'd incurred for being a right fucking wisecrack sometimes, son. I stayed quiet.

It wasn't until I got into bed each night that the strange thing would happen. I'd be drifting off, not having done much of note during the day, and would start to think about Miss Lee.

I'd never once thought about her all the time I was away from Tammersford. It therefore seemed odd at first, that while thoughts of my mother, or Benny across the street, or his parents, Mr and Mrs Lloyd who manned the auction room, or even my father, would merely induce a greyish indifference, my throat should tighten at her memory alone.

Instead of my mother raking leaves, for instance, and greeting me with a curt "hello, William," I'd see Miss Lee crouched on the floor, her tiny white ankles just visible under her dress. I'd then recall her before she was ill, when she'd clack through the assembly hall before morning registration and all the boys and I would stop what we were doing and watch. She always wore something lilac or pink, even in winter, and if one of the boys made a cheeky remark she'd say, "settle down, now, settle down," but she'd smile and blush and I always liked how her cheeks matched the colour of her blouse, as though she'd planned it that way.

My father had met her on parents' evening and joked that our car was older than she was. When I told her that she went very pink and said "Oh, Will." I was so worried I'd offended her that I really got my head down in Art, and the proof of the pudding would be in the upcoming spring exams. Only the Friday before Whitsuntide Miss Lee wasn't to be there, and – worse for us – we were to fall under the tutelage of Mrs Sparrow: Head of Department.

From that point onwards, Miss Lee wasn't to be there every third Friday, nor the occasional Monday morning that followed. When she didn't come back after the summer we all presumed something serious had happened, and I'd spend the afternoons up on the moorland near Mason's Forest. When asked if anything was the matter, my throat was hot and dry as a pottery kiln.

She was back in October, and I remembered wanting to ask someone if they thought her hair looked different.

Mornings here were better. I didn't think about Miss Lee, or anyone else in Tammersford. The early March sun did not breed gloomy thoughts like the damp, heavy nights. I found that she barely entered my head, even as I traced my old walks across the moorland.

Rather, it would always happen that, as soon as I switched off the television and dimmed the bedside lamp, her small body would loom into view, crumpled on the frost-lined tarmac, adults swarming around her telling us to get back, get back. I hadn't heard her fall, which I supposed was testament to her composure and grace; just a strange piping of student cries that heralded her collapse. "It wasn't expected," people had said. As far as they understood it, she was on the mend.

I sketched an oak tree that day, and refused to eat the stew my mother had made.

On the fifth night, I wondered if seeing Miss Lee on paper would help extricate her from my nightly thoughts. I made my way into town the next morning for charcoal and laid paper. It was a quiet road, the one that dove (and there was nothing gradual about the descent) into the centre. The town planners had done well, I thought, to quicken the build-up, for there was little to be found that was worthy of anticipation.

Grey buildings slouched against one another, pained and higgledy-piggledy, some drawing further pity with scars that attested an unpleasant history: smashed windows, vacant insides. Those that still yielded activity seemed to tug against the pace of their frequenters, as a sulky child might tug on its mother's arm. People moved quickly and looked mostly at the floor. The empty bandstand in the square, a Kaaba of ruin and waning interest, had procured a brownish sheen since I was last here. I made my purchases, and retreated.

Up on the moorland, the air settled sluggishly into ponds, swallowing the spindly stuff of bushes and reeds. But before the light left, I realised that drawing the old mill and the river was more settling for the mind than my original idea. If my father had been here, he would have told me I had what he called a real eye for detail, because I'd taken care to include even the old tyres at the foot of the mill, which most people would likely have missed. I brought the charcoal across the page then dithered into frenzied strokes, back and forth, back and forth; I signed off with a page-wide smudge to capture the heavy air.

My thoughts were on my father during the walk home. Crossing the station platform on my way back to the Cockerel, I came across the same old man in the grey suit, and was instantly reminded of how my father's penchant for solitude seemed to jar with his unbidden likeability. Having no form of cover for my sketches, I was forced to hold them inside my jumper as it started to rain. I wished I'd brought a jacket, and made a short remark to that effect.

The old man chuckled in agreement. He used to be a bus driver, and a joiner before that, born in Tammersford, of course, born and raised, and was I a local man? And could he see my pictures?

I told him yes, well, I was. The old man leant against a streetlight and lit a cigar. The tip glowed, and I could see blotches on his face; purple and red. He examined my pictures and said I really ought to sketch with the mill behind me, not in front. He told me you only really get a sense of how the forest feeds into the town if you look down on it from the mill, because from most other angles it's just a green blur. I thanked him, and he nodded. Born and raised here, me, he said, as I made my way towards the Cockerel.

I noticed Miss Lee in her office with a bunch of flowers as I was passing one day, and stopped, perhaps to say something. Or

## The Tammersford Lot

just smile. She had her back to me as she placed the flowers in a vase, and she drank in their scent, savouring the moment – I supposed – a feat always best executed by the dying. I smelled what I learned years later must have been a Jericho rose, or similar. But a door swung open at the end of the corridor, and I repealed my intentions. It would be the last time I saw her alive.

In place of a greeting, the old man asked me if I'd managed to get up there yet, son. Up to the mill, he meant. I told him that I had been sorting out my affairs in the town that day. He took a long puff on his cigar and let the smoke tumble out of his mouth.

The view won't be there forever, he said.

The evening had manifested in its usual dour manner and it started to rain as we spoke. I said, I haven't really had the chance today. My mother passed away two months ago, and I have to start putting things in order.

The old man asked about my father, so I told him he'd died last winter and that he may have known him: William Garrett. The old man shook his head and asked if he was born in the town. I told him he certainly was, sir, and as he turned to set down his cigar I wondered if the sir was necessary or if I'd just become a creature of habit.

Go up to the bloody mill tomorrow, the old man said. He pulled his coat around him tightly. That forest's been there as long as I can remember, but it won't always be. The council will fell it soon enough, you mark my words. Soon as someone says it's no longer fit for purpose.

I said, I'll go, sir.

There was a set of old chalks in the pub: red, blue and green. I placed them in my pocket alongside some charcoal and a few sheets of folded paper. I told the landlord I wanted to extend my stay by a week, threw on the only thick jacket I had and took breakfast in the town centre, coffee and a teacake. As the will was straightforward as far as documents of that nature go (I was to inherit the family home while my parents' savings were to go to the local dogs' refuge; I had not been there when my mother passed away, whereas Libby and Baxter had), I had more time than originally expected to spend on the moorland. With only a short space of time to get the house surveyed and up on the market, I determined to use the day to successfully mourn Miss Lee, then go about my business.

The sun was fuzzy behind the mist. I sat for forty minutes looking down from the foot of the mill and first sketched the forest, then, too attached to my original project to abandon her altogether, drew Miss Lee as part of the view.

She appeared somewhat out of place, of course; her pink blouse and high heels rendered her somewhat lost. Sketching her form was both necessary and uncomfortable, as it had been two days ago, but I did find solace in drawing the forest's trilateral lineation, which began with firs and ended in birch, and the way the town grew around its point in roughly concentric circles. It was grey against the forest, and greyer still against Miss Lee's clothes; its skyline dragged low and solemn across the horizon.

As night fell, I saw the old man propped against the streetlight next to the platform. I'd come to expect him there. I told him I'd been up to the mill, and when he asked to see my sketches, I described a young lady on the moorland and how I'd thought it a nice touch to include her in the piece. Her pink blouse was smudged; Miss Lee looked like she was running.

The old man raised an eyebrow (I struggled to discern approval or otherwise), and remarked that you didn't really get her sort up on the moorland. He asked, was she local?

I said, I don't know, sir. Didn't speak to her.

She looks like she's in the wrong gear, the old man said, for the moorland, like.

Perhaps, I replied.

The wrong gear, indeed. He cleared his lungs forcefully. He said, I had a son your age, you know.

Ah, yes? At once, it seemed plausible that he might even know Miss Lee. Might he recognise her? Might he have once joked about her at parents' evening, paid a little too much attention to her pink blouse? I felt a sensation long repressed, long buried, like my tragedies were never purely my own.

He was a good lad, my son, the old man went on. He wasn't half bad at art, either, and he could fashion you just about anything out of wood, soon as look at you. He got mixed up with the wrong crowd, that's all. The wrong girl, really, I should say. But happen there's plenty who'll say he was a rotter from the start.

A palsy of yellowy fog had seeped over the highest point of the moorland. Knowing by now that it would turn to rain once it reached the town, I made to leave.

Judging by that jacket, I imagine you've seen things yourself, son.

I nodded. I felt we were on the point of familiarity, and longed to be a stranger again.

You got a girlfriend? A wife? Kids?

The old man lit his cigar and I watched as it burned. I said no, and his thick eyelids lowered.

There's a lot to be said, he mumbled, for that decision. A lot to be said. Love's the stuff, you know, but it's remembering you love them that's the tricky part. He said through smoke, there's plenty who forget.

The old man tapped my drawings, and continued, No, son, just like our forest, it doesn't really last, doesn't love.

I knew what was coming.

Strapping young lad like you, though, you must have met someone special at one point or other.

The rain began, as promised, slowly at first, then with unequivocal intent. I looked down and affected a side-smile, as the young generally do well. I said, well, you know.

A good answer, I thought as I bade him good evening. It told enough. After crossing the platform, I made a half-turn to see if he was still there, but only his cigar remained.

That same night, I thought about Miss Lee before going to sleep, and even went on to dream about her for the first time. She was following me as I walked across the moorland, a chalk and charcoal figure, but each time I spoke to her she'd turn and run, her pink blouse billowing and a wilted bunch of roses clutched tightly to her chest.

## **Dress Lady**

I notice people all the time, now. I home in on the details, mostly, and by that I mean how jolly they look, or weary, or how their coat swings down from tight, bracketed shoulders. I count the colours they wear – red, brown, an amber ring – and find it jarring when sallow faces sink beneath a cosseting of exotic hues.

And eyes. Grey verging on silver, still then flicking, darting, like trout suddenly roused to movement; or deep, brown, midwife eyes, the type that say, now, now dear.

What might take me beyond the act of noticing someone is how I see them in relation to myself (note, I have never articulated anything to that effect; it is only now that I think about it that I can track patterns). Somebody will hold my attention for a little while longer if they show me either what I ought to be by now, or what I'm glad I didn't end up as. Both go against what the dominant narrative would have us do – live and let live, and so on – but if my commute yields the odd human benchmark that I can use to assess who I've become, I'll take it.

Dress lady is one such benchmark. She's on my train every day. Courtesy of the beautiful wrap-around dresses she used to wear in summer, she acquired a nickname, but with warmongering eastern winds careering in, along with snow, we're all in coats, now, of course. The rain, at least, is occasional.

Mine is navy, and cumbersome, but not deliberately so. Warped and compressed, it looks like a deflated airbed next to her neat, seemingly brand new trench. The collars of my pink blouses always stick out and clash with the colour until I feel embarrassed. Ugly, in fact. When the rain does fall, it falls in pools, while engineers in wet neon crouch to fix the tracks. Somehow, Dress Lady always seems to stay dry.

She's older than me. I think, much older. She is slight, and very pretty, or at least she was once, and her short, red hair (presumably dyed) parts manageably to divulge deep, blue-green eyes. I think about my hair, or lack thereof.

When she rides the train alone, her countenance is steady, serious, and gives away little. Yet she'll often start typing handwritten notes as soon as she sits down and then I'll notice her head dart from paper to screen, frenetic as an eyeball. When she rides the train with colleagues, she smiles often, but it's a smile – buttressed by a volley of encouraging nods – that merely keeps up with conversation; I've yet to see a smile that comes from within, that engages the eyes.

Some people give away everything by way of their expression, or their walk. That they cried when they got their ears pierced, or that they'd wait patiently while a street magician made them a sausage dog balloon, is all evident in a twitchy disposition and a slow, lolloping gait. Much as I'd like my own character to remain covert, I imagine my train conduct lays me out like a map. But dress lady reveals nothing. For her every inscrutable look, I'm visibly worried, or curious, or annoyed; for her every expressionless smile, mine conveys joy, or surprise, or pitying apologism for the barely-veiled manner of other, more readable commuters.

I have never spoken to Dress Lady. I wish I could inject some kind of narrative into this piece, but there is none. I saw her in town once, wearing jeans, buying things, and I'd hoped that her softened appearance might induce a gentler character. By that I mean I thought she might have acknowledged me when we crossed paths, but there was nothing. I felt a fool for smiling at her, and quickly retracted it.

And it just so goes that, during the life I have left, I would like to learn whether such reticence is a question of effort, of force, and – in which case – does it ever stop feeling that way? Will I ever resist the urge to swap a double-breasted Mac for a duffle coat, in spite of the wind? Will people's dithering attempts to let me on the train before them one day fail to elicit

## The Tammersford Lot

a grin, and a giggly acceptance of their offer? And, if so, is such a transformation really one that I seek, or, like the rickety train that carries us to work, will I continue to traverse new ground, but remain – if a little weather beaten – basically unchanged?

Today, work was a drag. People are kind, but only to my failing body. They would never condone my thoughts. They'd say, be glad! You're on the mend! Life! With the tip of my shoe, I trace part of the yellow line on the platform. Life. Two men emerge, staggering somewhat, but silent, from the Boar's Head. A heavy bird rocks the old lamp, and beyond the tunnel, the train's headlights defy the evening darkness. Life. I pull my coat in at the neck, and my hat firmly down. The small crowd inches forward, dress lady and all, and old dreams cry out as if from a sea beneath the tracks.

## Clara's Home Job

Although she was due to colour her hair (a messy affair, no matter how languid her rubbing movements), choosing to redecorate the bathroom had been a good decision. Granted, she hadn't yet found the source of the damp, but the walls which last week bore a surfeit of moss-green rosettes now glowed an acceptable shade of white. Peony sized, the blooms of mould had encroached on her morning meditations, as visual incongruities always had.

Her thoughts had been all over the place last week. She had been trying out chairs in the auction room, a task that she eventually had to abandon when the precipitate rebukes of (the somewhat haggard) Mrs Lloyd – 'Madame, Madame, with respect, you must not sit on that if you've been out in the rain!' – threw her concentration entirely. Now her mind was exactly still; hadn't she been preparing all weekend to immerse herself fully in the colouring process?

She opened the bathroom window, closed the door behind her and let the warm evening air pass over her skin. If she had wanted to name its scent she might have said heather, but she wondered – given her distance from the moorland, and given that it was far too early for heather – if such a thought had merely been encouraged by a slight wink of lilac in the paintwork. Such a hue was unexpected, so she turned her chunk of amethyst stone-side up, thinking it may have refracted the light, or something. Lilac or not, it really didn't make that much difference, because the bathroom was more pristine than it had been in years and the new tiles above the sink were as straight as breakwaters.

In fact, her only concern at this stage was whether she still had reason to keep the four hair dye bottles from the first year she'd chosen to 'go red'; Amber, Copper, Medium Burgundy and Burgundy, each lasting around three months, had proved a fitting nod to the seasons and a pattern from which she had never had cause to deviate. And wasn't she – Clara Holmes – always reminded of what an excellent choice she made when – at the turn of the season – her colleagues would compliment her newly-dyed hair? And the bottles were so beautiful (though slightly flecked with white paint); like tiny vials of anointing oil with round, cabochon heads. They didn't make them like they used to.

Delving into her shopping bag, she pulled out the purchase she'd made that morning: a bottle of Amber to mark the start of spring. Slowly, she lowered herself to her knees and began rinsing her hair over the bathtub. Somehow she'd managed to forget the official start of the season and had been very busy at work for most of April; it was not like her to be colouring well into May. Yet though the Burgundy had faded, she hadn't let herself go like some of the girls (what knowledge an inch or two could reveal: she now understood that a few of them were all but entirely white).

She worked the dye into a lather only as fast as her joints would allow, and paused to experience the suds as they popped like little geysers in her hair. She couldn't help but grin as she imagined how her whole persona would soon undergo a sea change; why, even her voice might, for a time, lose its hoarse, self-lacerating tone. Though she had never been one for pithy remarks or cheap pot shots, she imagined herself in the auction room tomorrow morning, face to face with Mrs Lloyd (how she had it all, that woman), and began to half whisper, half spit a torrent of reproaches that she had been chewing on all week. Each would knock Mrs Lloyd sideways with the force of a heavy desk globe. She passed a moment in which she didn't allow these thoughts, her hands submerged in the warm, marbled bathwater and her head pulled back, eyes closed, in a smiling, upward exaltation, before proceeding to rinse again.

The last two times she'd dyed she'd sat by the radiator, leaning into its heat to let her hair dry. Sometimes, she'd run her fingers over the jagged surface of the amethyst as she waited. But today, she decided to sit downwind of the warm spring evening breeze, and positioned herself against the jamb of the window. How relaxed she was; such peace! She would have felt wholly undisturbed were it not for the exciting prospect of seeing her renewed reflection in the steamy mirror. Her hair was only half dry when she used her sleeve to wipe away the steam.

Only she – Clara Holmes – had not imagined the long ribands of orange that had seeped down her forehead as though from some ruptured lesion. Nor could she ever have foreseen what a frightfully pale result a few extra weeks' negligence could procure. In the light, her roots seemed to have taken on no colour at all.

She couldn't have let more than a few seconds pass before closing the window and draining the bathwater. A faint smell of damp seemed to creep into the room. Was it just her, or had bulbs of dark green begun to reappear on the newly-painted walls? She pinned her hair up, and in that very same moment chose to give it until next week before deciding about the dye bottles; seven sleeps should do it, she thought, and she might even consider keeping the amethyst face down too, concluding – quite resolutely – that she preferred how its wheaten exterior fit better with the rest of the room.

## **Young Codgers**

In Florian's, there was nowhere to be alone. There was no outhouse to gather your thoughts, and the awning above the porch did little to shield the smokers from the elements. The road in front of the bar – the one that snaked its way from the moorland to Tammersford town centre – lay in scoops and humps, embattled by potholes, as it ended its route. You didn't want to be taking a stroll, clearing your head, after the streetlamps went out.

Douglas watched his wife Molly as she left. She told him not to be late and fumbled with the hem of her shirt sleeves.

'Alright darling, alright. I shall see you at home later,' he said. His words were indistinct, and instead of embracing her, he leaned on her somewhat. It occurred to him how remarkable she looked tonight, though she wouldn't know it, and would surely never appreciate his telling her. When he first fell for Molly, there had been a sequence to things: the eyes, the lips, then the huge smile – which was a real reckoning since he had supposed her sultry demeanour incapable of expressing real cheer – and it had taken a moment or two to process the sight, like when one sees the moon in daylight, or a crocus in January.

The music in Florian's put Douglas out. He would never have come here given the choice. Molly knew, he thought. Molly knew this wasn't his sort of place, just like she knew that when he cracked a joke in company he was uncomfortable, and when he told someone that he hoped he would cross paths with them again, it meant he probably hoped he wouldn't. He finished his drink and told the bartender he'd have the same again.

'Evening, Mr Lloyd.' Kate stood right behind Douglas and breathed the words into his ear. She smelled of peaches. 'I knew you'd be here. I knew you couldn't resist the lure of Florian's.'

She had a way of drawing her laughter back behind her teeth so that it sounded nasal and deliberately stifled; never repressed.

Douglas turned to face her. She wore a tight, green dress and a pair of pearl earrings that dangled from delicate silver chains; her white skin bore a delicate, gossamer-like quality. In fact, where the bar was brightest it was almost lilac, like the casing of a bubble caught by the light.

'Aren't you going to say hello?' she asked.

'Of course. I was just wondering what to compliment first, the earrings or the dress.' Douglas kissed her once on the cheek and asked her if she would like something to drink.

'I'd like a red wine, please.'

'Red wine? I thought it'd be, I don't know, vodka with something green in it. I'm sure you were drinking some luminous garbage at the rugby finals in April.'

She leaned against him and pressed her hands into his sides. 'Or maybe you were just looking for the green light.' Douglas eased away from her, seeking the barman's attention. 'Come on, I noticed you looking at me that day. You couldn't wait to come over and talk to me.'

'Hadn't seen you in years, that's all. Couldn't believe how much you were looking like your mum, these days.'

'You said Florian's wasn't really your scene. Why'd you come?'

'Well every other bar's got the footie on, and I'm not really a football kind of bloke.'

Kate moved in closer again, this time winding her arm around his middle. She exhaled, and paced her words. 'I don't believe you.'

'Hi, yeah, can I get another pint, please, and a red wine for the lady?'

Her voice was higher, this time. 'Just because I look like my mum, it doesn't mean I'm a lady, you know. You must think I'm older than I am.'

'Why? How old are you exactly?'

## The Tammersford Lot

'I told you at the rugby match – when I was ready to leave Sunday school, your lad had just started to attend. Our Sunday school teacher was so square, a real fuddy-duddy, she didn't know what to do with your Ben, he was such a rascal; couldn't stand anyone being a bit different. And she certainly didn't know what to do with moi.' She paused. 'But I bet you would, Douglas. I bet you'd know just what to do with me.'

'See, Kate, that...that's still a little too cryptic for me, that age puzzle.' Douglas laughed, but he thought immediately of his son, and how long it had been since he'd seen Molly smile. He lowered his gaze to the bar.

'Oh, I'm sorry, Douglas. I didn't think, I-'

'No, that's ok, Kate. It's not like he's...dead.'

'How is he these days? I mean, it must be just awful knowing...'

'He's much the same, really, much the same. Molly and I have a sort of shift pattern going. It fits around our work lives. And we've hired a carer for Saturday mornings if Molly does the auction and I'm called into the office.'

'I always thought you were too young to have a grown man for a son. You're what I'd call a young codger.' She wrinkled her nose and laughed; it was a nice laugh, Douglas thought, like china on china. When she was a child, he was sure it was her that used to roar when she scored a rounder.

'Codger? I've only just seen in fifty. And Molly was about forty five, last time I checked!

'Isn't your wife's age something you should know?'

'Well, yes, as a matter of fact, I suppose it is. But it took all of me to get her to join me for a drink tonight. Can't remember the last time we celebrated a birthday.'

'Just as well you came here, then. All company in Florian's is good company.' Kate brought her glass to her lips. The wine's oaky aroma doused her girlish perfume and Douglas found himself drawn to that contrast, that chasmal vale between womanhood and late adolescence.

'That's what I hear,' he said. As he drank, he watched her. Her earrings danced in the light.

It was late. Douglas closed the front door behind him. He thought, if there had been little prospect of solitude in Florian's, here, the opportunity was everywhere. He held onto the side of the sofa to steady himself, and shouted up to his wife. His low, rumbling call would have been unfamiliar to her.

'Douglas? Is everything alright? What on earth is the time?'

Molly entered the living room and turned on the light. Douglas had poured a port for himself and a brandy for her.

'Sit down,' he said. His words were slow, heavy.

'What's the matter, Douglas? Is it Benny? Have you been up with him?'

'Sit down, Molly.'

'Now you tell me Benny's ok, or–'

'Benny's fine. He's fine. Molly, I want you to sit, sit down, and I want you to hear me.'

He steered her into the groove in the sofa that for too long had born witness to their sedentary existence.

'When you left Florian's, I bumped into Kate Drew.'

'Jane and Terry's daughter? She's trouble, she is, and so is her brother. He got put away last month.'

'Yes, she's trouble, she's chaos, but I didn't so much bump into her as, well, go to the place where I knew...where I knew I'd find her.'

Molly said nothing. She drank her brandy. A little came away and trailed down the side of her mouth, so she dabbed at it with her dressing gown sleeve, and with her thumb and fingertips began to rub the sleeves' hems like she was working raw pastry. A red line over the moorlands told her it was nearly morning. She stood up, straightened the rug with her feet, looked at her husband – taking care to avoid his eyes – then at the mantelpiece, which she noticed had accrued a little dust.

'Nothing happened, Mol.' Douglas grabbed his wife's hand. 'But I wanted you to know, you have to know that there was...there was a part of me that wanted, I don't know, something more than - I mean, we never do anything, anymore, do we? You and I?'

Molly shook herself loose. 'Silly old fool. I'm going to turn Benny,' she said. 'Don't follow me.'

'That's why I went there, you know. Because you stopped loving me. I'm not entirely stupid. And you know what else? I'm a sensitive guy. I have feelings, you know. I have feelings. I-'

'Drunken old fool. You'll wake Benny. You can sleep here tonight. Here...'

She threw him a blanket. Benny's downstairs blanket. It was still soiled.

Douglas clenched the port glass. He couldn't bear her silence because it permitted him nothing. With an argument, he could steer the marriage to its rightful conclusion, but in all the months he'd been thinking things over, he'd never once anticipated that her reticence could extend even to a situation like this.

The red dawn had given way to a blue June morning. Molly would have to come down eventually, and Douglas considered telling her that he couldn't help it, but that he had enjoyed Kate's passionate grip, the way she exhaled words and blew them into his heart. But goading her clearly did no good. Perhaps he would have to do it. Perhaps he'd have to address the other thing. The thing they passed between them, like the stale air they shared when the nights were warm, but never felt cause to mention; the thing that, if Douglas ever did have to explain it in its contemptible entirety, was, by and large, Molly's headlong dive into midlife without so much as a nod to her former self, driven in her trajectory by a son whose injuries were, if not exactly convenient, then certainly useful.

## **Before the Shopping Trip**

When the coffees arrived, India cupped her mother's hand in hers and told her she'd heard that, out of all the tearooms in town – or those remaining, at least – the cakes here really were the best.

Her mother, who appeared to wince at the upward inflection in India's remark, did not withdraw her hand, but within its casing let her fingers lie limp. With her free hand, she lifted her drink and blew lightly across its surface, her small mouth tight like a flute player's. She replied, with a sigh clumsily shoehorned into her delivery, that they looked a little dry to her. And she didn't see why they had to bother with Tammersford for shopping, when for sale signs and boarded up windows were the order of the day.

A high ding signalled the arrival of three more customers. They were discussing an unusual mist on the edge of Mason's Forest, and the young waiter informed them it was the result of a heat inversion. To inspect the sky immediately above them, India had to lean forward across the table, causing the light to fall in a small plash over her face. Her skin was always as smooth as an egg, a starkly apparent quality on account of the midday glare, and the way she drew her pale eyebrows into perfect arches was the only feature that distinguished her from her mother, whose linear, slightly rumpled brow pared two bright, violet eyes.

India sat back in her chair. 'I do like spending time with you,' she said. 'Isn't it nice, just the two of us, sometimes?'

'No you don't. You like arguing with me.' India's mother pierced her daughter's cupped hands with an accusatory forefinger, which she began to brandish as she had done when India was a child. 'If you watch these television debates, you'll notice that they discuss–'

'Well I–'

'No listen- that they discuss issues; they don't insult each other. You know, Indie, I'm sure I didn't bring you up to sign off arguments with such personal attacks.'

'I'm sorry. I feel all embarrassed now. I really didn't mean to hurt your feelings.'

'You called me vulgar.'

'I meant your views were vulgar.'

'Well, your tone was most brutish.' Something about her own tone was rather misleading; it suggested neither offence taken nor defence intended. Rather, her articulation bore the tone of a vainglorious prefect: patronisingly instructive. With her free hand, she squeezed India's briefly, made a brusque sweeping motion and insisted they heard no more about it.

Two new customers entered the cafe. India only half watched as they sat down at the neighbouring table. Complaining about a strange smoke this time, the pair seemed to attract the interest of the young waiter. India spread her hands behind her neck and cast her gaze towards the ceiling.

'I resent your calling me brutish,' she said at last. 'And I don't like arguing with you. It's just...I mean how do you expect me to react when you say things like that? Am I to simply hold my tongue every time I disagree with you?'

'Well, a little common courtesy wouldn't go amiss,' her mother replied. 'I'd never expect such rudeness from any of my congregation and I certainly wouldn't expect it from you!'

'Your congregation? Mum, you're only a Sunday school teacher, for Christ's sake!' India exhaled slowly. Her eyes followed the waiter as he stepped outside.

'The thing is, Mother, you know my views on the matter,' she said. 'To remain quiet every time you judge someone like that would be anathema to me. And I am a courteous person, you know I am. Never gave you any trouble during my teens, I mean we never really argued, did we? It's just that sometimes I can't-'

'Ah but you don't let the other person speak, you see, Indie. You get very personal about things, and so flipping analytical, and then you strut off in a sulk! Now if you were on one of those panel shows on television, to strut off in a temper would be considered a very poor do indeed. You must learn to appreciate that sometimes, peoples' views may be different to your own, but that you should learn to respect them nonetheless.'

'Well I respect you, you know I do. I just don't – I can't – respect the views you–'

'Ah...ah...see now, Indie, I think you've become extremely disrespectful since your teenage years, and you probably haven't even noticed. But I've noticed.' India's mother waved her finger once more, a gesture that was at once more fitting given the thinly-veiled frustration in her voice. 'All you seem to do lately is answer back; making sure you always have the last word! I expected far more decorum from the daughter I raised; from the daughter I fed and clothed and for whom I provided shelter for far longer a time than legally necessary. Not that that was a problem, of course. All I ask is that you don't continue to spoil what has been a lovely day with your gracelessness. Now, let's enjoy our coffees before they go cold.'

'But Mother, won't you concede that there's a difference between disrespecting your views and disrespecting you? I really don't mean to spoil this day but I doubt you could even give me one example of a time when–'

'I was wrong, totally wrong, folks!' India jumped as the waiter hurried back through the door. He had short, brown hair and long, grasshopper limbs. 'I must jettison my previous hypothesis, ladies and gentlemen, in favour of the latest on mistgate!'

India's mother nodded her head towards him. Coffee in hand, she said: 'Now he's a case in point if ever I saw one, Indie. Surely you can see what I mean by...indiscrete.'

'The mist from the moors is in fact smoke,' he continued, calling over his shoulder as he cut through a lemon sponge cake. 'I've just been told they've clipped down a few trees from the forest and they're burning them out near the mill. A chap outside told me they're clearing a space for some car park they're wanting to build, or something. Nothing to worry about, nothing to worry about, though apparently the smell might linger until the evening. And if anyone notices a bright flame, it's birch they're burning.'

India pressed down on her temples and stared at a stain on the table cloth. 'I resent that comment, mother, I really do,' she said quietly. 'He's simply trying to be helpful.'

'Oh look, Indie, see there you go again,' she replied, poking her daughter's forearm. In her wake, she left a rich waft of perfume redolent of lavender and petitgrain. 'I insist that you let it lie now. And I don't know if this is a fair assumption but this...system you seem to have developed of talking back, putting people down, sulking and then massaging their egos is possibly what drove Mark away. I mean save your soft soaping for the bathtub, for heaven's sake! Now clearly I don't know what goes on behind closed doors but I wouldn't be a good mother if I didn't make these links. Can you imagine what things would have been like if I had talked to your father in such a manner? Can you just imagine?'

India's mother took a sip of coffee, glanced at her daughter and plucked a sachet of white sugar from the jar. She stirred her drink a little more than was necessary and took a moment to gaze out of the window. Outside, people were waiting for a bus that would either come late, or not at all. Their jeans were scuffed at the hem, trawled unwittingly over a spree of grey and white chewing gum.

'Now I don't suppose you watched that programme about JFK last night?' she asked. 'It was a bit like a whodunit really; lots of conflicting evidence! You would have liked it, Indie, you were always a whizz at solving puzzles. They were saying that Harvey Oswald fellow might not have been responsible after all; there may have been more than one rifle involved. A lot of witnesses that stood a fair way from where Oswald had shot from reported smelling cordite from a gun, and they wouldn't have smelled that if it had come from Oswald's firearm because it simply wouldn't have carried.'

India didn't respond. Instead, she regarded her mother with a vacant look and then, having nodded solemnly at the close of the story, proceeded to gulp down her coffee in one. She wiped her mouth with the back of her thumb while her mother frowned slightly but said nothing. They passed a minute in silence.

'Why don't you let me buy you one of those cakes, Indie?' India's mother summoned the waiter with a curt, beckoning motion. 'How about the lemon one, shall we get you the lemon one? You said these cakes were supposed to be good. Yes, we'll have a slice of the lemon cake, young man, and another round of coffees. Bring a little jug of single cream, if you will.' She took one final sip of her drink and signalled for the waiter to take it.

'It might be early June but there's certainly a nip in the air,' she continued, shivering emphatically as the waiter held the door for two more customers. 'I do hope it warms up before our shopping trip.'

Like two sparks, her violet eyes flashed in the midday light, a glaring beam of white that had her and India squinting. Above the aroma of freshly-brewed coffee India caught a hint of the smoke from outside. She considered its fumy, somewhat brackish odour then watched as her mother caught the same air. As the waiter closed the door and told the parting customers they were very welcome, India encouraged the odour's drift by gathering it towards her with a cupped hand. This time, she inhaled it pointedly, gazed through narrowed eyes out of the window, inhaled again, and asked her mother if she thought cordite smelled anything like that.

## **Good People**

That was his mate's parents' old house, that. James passed it often, but he didn't make the connection every time. Sometimes, the bus lurched too much, and he had to sit back and pinch his lips together to stop the vomit coming out. Not that it ever had, mind. You know when you just over worry about something? Sometimes, he was thinking about work, specifically the customers whom he forced himself not to despise, or whether or not he had closed the pantry door properly. It was always swinging open.

The pear tree in the front garden was still tall, but then it will have grown since he was a child. The patio, on the other hand, had shrunk. How did they ever play penalty shoot-outs in that? James, granted, never really put much effort in, much to the annoyance of his mate's dad, who was, save for one son, laden with four daughters and their dollies. What a prick he used to be. No, not a prick - just small minded. And he couldn't remember if they had had a mirror in their front room, like this new family clearly had. James had been drunk for the first time in that house, and he had looked in a big mirror and laughed, slowly, a sort of mixture of squeaks and honks, at his own reflection. But which mirror? He recalled he had been alone. He had smelled aftershave and potpourri. So chances are it wasn't in the front room.

The bus, at least, was driving slowly this evening, and the temperature – thank goodness – was mild for mid summer. James kept reaching for the stick of dark chocolate he had stowed in his bag, but it wasn't really what he fancied. It was more a sort of requirement, these days; in fact he didn't think he even enjoyed it that much anymore. He really should have brought something fruity, something like a boiled sweet, sweet but sour, first, perhaps; something you felt like you'd earned. Besides, chocolate on the bus might have brought on the vomit feeling. Past his mate's parents' old house, they pulled up outside the college. James thanked the driver, and thought about how badly he wished he'd bought some sour peaches.

It was a fine building, the college. It used to be an army college, and the gates were high and gilded. James adored the old library, and would sit in the Law section before class started, in the same chair – always – to take in the heady smell of books. People might have thought he was studying Law. He certainly looked the type, all tall and thin with round glasses and a solemn look, but then he would have been at a university, wouldn't he, and not in Tammersford, in a sixth form college, in the evening, after work?

Mrs Dale, the librarian, was there tonight. James said, 'Good evening, Mrs Dale. Isn't the weather picking up?'

She opined, 'It's been just lovely this week.'

'Really nice, yes.'

She didn't mention the incident.

'Have you recovered, then, after your trauma with the photocopier?' James asked.

'Sorry, have I what? Oh yes, heck, was that a week ago? Do you know, time's going that fast. Yes, well I wouldn't go as far as to call it a trauma, but I'm certainly glad you were there to help.'

'I was only too happy to, Mrs Dale. Have a nice evening. Hope you don't get too many tricky requests!'

An interesting sign off, James thought. It wasn't like the library was busy. Actually, an awkward conversation altogether. He really didn't need to bring up the photocopying incident. He'd heard the machine whirring for over ten minutes, gone to alert Mrs Dale – who was over in Psychology – and together they had spotted that she'd requested 300 copies as opposed to 30. He had told her how to cancel it: job done. Finito. Nothing to write home about. Being a Good Person, James had already learned, should be seamless, glossed over, brushed away with the flick of a wrist. Ah, it was nothing. Come on, don't mention it. He knew plenty of Good People,

## The Tammersford Lot

and they would never have relayed a time when they had helped someone, let alone remind the recipient of their good fortune. Imagine Tony Giuliani doing that. Imagine.

He was there, was Tony, when James went over to the coffee machine.

'This coffee really is rancid, isn't it?' James said.

'Well I usually take decaf, so I wouldn't know.' He wasn't handsome, Tony Giuliani, but he was what you'd call rugged, a Ret Butler type; someone your Grandma would have liked.

'Decaf? I had you down as a man after the real thing.'

Tony Giuliani laughed; a two-hum affair. 'Come on, lad,' Tony nudged his head towards the machine, 'what rancid coffee can I get you?'

'Oh, that's really good of you, cheers. I'll have a cappuccino, please.'

How did he do it? Was he just naturally nice? James would never have thought to do that. He would have made small talk, most likely, and bought a coffee for himself. He wondered if Tony sat for five minutes every morning (sometimes ten) and meditated on how he'd do good that day, how he'd make someone's existence a little more bearable. He wondered if Tony ever got it wrong, or – when an opportunity presented itself – simply forgot, or something. James couldn't see it. He thought, perhaps he's perpetually drunk.

'See you in class,' James said.

'Yep.' Effortless.

French classes were alright. James wasn't much of a linguist, but he tried his best, and the pace was a bit more to his liking since the swots had moved on. Before the course started – over a year ago now – he had made a calculated decision based on the following criteria:

French:
Makes you sound cultured.
Makes you sound sexy.

Makes it permissible to say to phrases like *plus ça change, plus c'est la meme chose* which, particularly at work, enables you to curry favour with the more educated customers.

Would be useful for travel in North Africa, if ever he decided to go.

Would serve as a good base if he were to take up another romance language, such as Spanish, perhaps, or Italian. Italian, probably.

Was on Wednesday evenings, which was when his housemate, Ryan, cooked for his girlfriend, and she was an insufferable human.

Ok, maybe not insufferable. She and he just...needed to find a way of relating. That was the sort of thing Tony might say. James looked at him across the classroom. Yes. Yes, he could see him saying something like that. He'd never use the word insufferable to describe someone.

The teacher, Madame Wellesley – English, by all accounts, and so brutally so that she had never smoked a cigarette, post-coital or otherwise, in her life – was rounding things up. She was frantic as ever – all disco arms – and clearly couldn't see that the more she wore herself out explaining the past perfect, the more the class switched off. James took a swig of cold coffee and finished the last of his chocolate, which he had been nibbling at secretly (an English French teacher would never permit chocolat in class) for over an hour. He felt that lovely buzz, the lovely buzz that gears one up to do a good thing. It wasn't that he couldn't do a good thing without the lovely buzz, but if it was there to be had. . .

James had spent his morning meditation going over what he'd say.

'Madame Wellesley-'

'Yes, James.'

'I just wanted to say, I just wanted to say that you're really good at explaining things. You're really good at what you do.'

'Oh, thank you, James. Thank you, that's really made my night, that has.'

'Well, I mean it. You always make everything…really clear.'

'What a lovely thing to say.'

Out of the corner of his eye, he thought he saw Tony Giuliani raise an eyebrow.

James was thankful that the bus ride home was just as calm as the one there. It was dark, now, so he didn't see his mate's parents' old house, though he may have noticed the pear tree had he looked towards the lamppost. Besides, he was distracted by a pregnant lady who had sat near the front. She looked unwell. She was very pale. Maybe he should ask her if she was alright? When the bus pulled up to the next stop, he thought, he might ask her if she was alright. The lady leaned really far forward. Hadn't anyone else noticed her? The bus slowed. The lady put a cupped hand to her mouth, and James felt his stomach lurch. He thought he could taste chocolate. He pushed the bell and ran to the door, ignoring the taste, avoiding her eyes. It would surely have been like the blind leading the blind, if he'd tried to help.

## Mrs Boden

When I was nine, my father handed in his notice at the local paper. The last report he had written dealt with the sentencing of a young woman whose identity had, until that point, been protected by a court order. I remember, quite clearly, him coming home that evening, seating himself in the low armchair, placing a cushion on his lap and declaring, 'Well, that's that, then.'

It only took him three weeks to find a new job – in September he was to begin a part-time copywriter's role about half-an-hour's car journey from Tammersford – and when people asked why he didn't work at the paper anymore, he'd throw his hands up, pause for a moment (that was the Italian in him) and tell them that writing nonsense about young ladies who allowed their children to develop scurvy without any whiff of perspective – or compassion – just wasn't who he was anymore. It just wasn't who he was!

During the weeks that my father was between jobs, he, my older sister and I attended four barbeques. I didn't remember having been to any the previous year, but my father had a lot of well-wishers, and that August temperatures had suddenly soared. My mother was on secondment from her bank's local branch to a start-up unit in Spain, and would ring us daily to compare the weather (it was hotter there, but with frequent storms). My father shared a beer with Jack Stag and Harry Narkissos and told them he loved her, but she was what he called a real creature of habit, even abroad. Harry Narkissos said there were ways of coping with that, if they knew what he meant, and I didn't know what he meant but the men laughed and said we do, Harry, we certainly do.

Naturally, all the hacks at the gatherings had a view on the unusual weather. My father was the most forthcoming with his. At Geoff Manby's barbeque he said, 'This heat is unbearable,

## The Tammersford Lot

though I do enjoy a juicy apple in August rather than having to wait 'til October. It's not quite as hot as my burger making skills, mind, and if anyone cares to take issue with that they ought to remember that I am also in charge of dispensing condiments, and ergo the extra spicy chilli sauce.' As an endnote he brandished a pair of tongues. Everybody laughed, and so did I; as a child with limited means of expression, that was my way of saying I was happy to be with him.

The summer Father left his job we'd walk home at night instead of driving. My sister Fran (a year my senior) said she'd asked what would happen if it got so hot that people would come to Tammersford for their holidays instead of Girona, where mum was. She told me that Father had simply asked her what she thought, a technique to which Fran often responded with the whetted interest of a philosopher but which left me feeling cheated.

Yet it was to be the quest for answers that eventually brought us closer as sisters, especially during the summers when the afternoons grew infernally hot and the air would pulsate above the asphalt. We complained about the heat on the walk home from Geoff Manby's. The afternoon had stagnated to become a heavy, orange evening; there was something almost compact about the air.

I remembered stopping at a twenty-four-hour garage because my father wanted coffee. He told us he wanted to wet his whistle for the memory game, a fixture we'd developed on the way home from the last barbeque. I watched him drum two fingers on the hot drinks machine, and he held his jaw with the other hand, frowning. He asked if decaf coffee was available to which the assistant replied no, unless he expected them to brew up in the staff room for him. He dithered a little before selecting a flat white, and I thought I heard him ask for strength under his breath.

'We're going to play a slightly different version of the memory game,' father said as we left the garage. We took the main street that circled down into the city, and he let us walk in the road as there were no cars after eleven. 'I'm going to say a poem, and I want you both to remember it.'

'But that's bor-ing,' Fran told him. 'We want to play the proper game.'

'There might be a prize in it,' he said, tapping his pocket.

'Sweets!' I yelled.

'They're only the peppermints he buys for the car, Carys,' said Fran. 'I bet he only gives us one each.'

'Every time the workmen pause,' he recited, 'the silence works me down-' I interjected with a request that my father confirm this, but he walked ahead and refused to heed me. 'I want to cross the tongue and teeth, but thought precludes the sound.'

Ever the sharper sibling, Fran cut in with a suggestion, pulling on father's forearm as she spoke.

'Can you tell us that story you made up about Mrs Boden?'

'No.'

'Oh go on. You haven't told it to us in ages!'

'Well how would you feel if you were Mrs Boden and children were demanding horrible stories about you?'

Fran looked as confused as I felt. She said, 'But she's not a real person. And you used to tell us. You used to tell us all the time.'

'I wouldn't say all the time, young lady.'

Father picked up the pace. The last of the sunlight had faded, and the streetlights cast thin, quill-like shadows on the road. I heard Fran groan. 'But we like that story,' she said, 'and you never tell us stories anymore.'

'Now that's not true,' my father replied, but it only took a few seconds' effort to remind him that it was.

'There was once a couple called Mr and Mrs Boden,' he sighed. 'They were newcomers in Tammersford so nobody knew much about them, and because they kept themselves to themselves, it remained that way for years.'

## The Tammersford Lot

Fran shook me playfully, her blue eyes widening in morbid delight. 'I love this story,' she whispered. I said I did too, though I ran up to my father and slid my hand into his.

'Until one day, a neighbour said she'd seen Mrs Boden with a child,' Father continued. 'She said she'd seen a little boy toddling round with her, so he can't have been a newborn, and though they stayed out of things, nobody thought it possible that the couple had kept the birth of a child a secret.

'Funnily enough, the little boy seemed to give Mrs Boden a reason to venture out more. While before she'd only be seen now and again – in the corner shop buying milk, perhaps, or tending to the flowers around the front fence – neighbours started to report seeing her once or twice a week. She'd most likely be found in the park, or strolling up near the crags on the moorland, always in a bright red coat.

'Local teenagers said they'd even been carol singing there, and that Mrs Boden had listened politely with the child on her hip, though she didn't offer a word in the way of praise and one of them thought she'd been crying.

'Mr Boden was still a mystery. People suspected he either worked nights or worked away, because he was seldom seen in daylight. Only the fathers who met in the pubs reported seeing him, and that was only once every few months.

'But it was through him that we found out the child had died. According to one of the fathers, Mr Boden had been down the Boar's Head yelping like a dog, wondering how his wife could have let this happen. Rumour had it that he ordered four double whiskeys and tried to get in his car to drive home, only the landlord managed to stop him. In the days that followed, people left flowers and cards on their doorstep, until the news spread that the child may have died as a result of neglect. Then the flowers stopped arriving.'

'What does neglect mean, again?' Fran asked.

'It's when somebody is ignored.'

'I like the next bit, it's scary,' she declared, and she clung to Father's arm, yanking it as she bounced along, chirping, 'Scary, scary, scary.'

Father walked on stoically. The night was still and we had reached a stretch of road where the streetlights were dimmer and yellower. Underfoot, it had become a little bumpy. We were on the descent toward the town centre and I suddenly felt the need to cling on tighter. Father continued:

'Then, a strange thing happened - Mr Boden disappeared entirely. Some said he'd joined the army; others said he'd died of a broken heart. His wife, though accused, was never convicted of anything, and quickly became a recluse in her own home.

'From that point, the house turned into a dilapidated ruin. The front garden became overgrown, ivy began to shroud the walls, and the flowers around the fence withered and died. It stood out like a sore thumb; you know how uniform houses in Tammersford are. Reports soon circulated of a soul-chilling, yearning wail coming from within the house at night – the only sign that Mrs Boden still lived there – though if anyone took the time to listen, they were met with a thick, almost palpable silence.

'One evening, a group of local boys was playing football on the street. One of them accidentally kicked the ball into the Bodens' garden, and because he was the youngest and most innocent looking, he was forced by the others to go and retrieve it.

'Assisted by an older boy, he climbed over the fence and began to scrabble around in the overrun garden. He gave them back the ball, though to his great dismay, the others – being boys of a cruel age – decided to run away, and sprinted the length of the street to the sound of the boy's reproachful groans.

'But they were swiftly followed by cries of a different nature.

'Having changed course upon hearing these cries, the boys returned to a deathly stillness. Save for the faint sound of a barking dog, the street was silent.

'They called the boy's name - nothing. It wasn't until one member of the group concluded that the boy must have been playing a hoax of his own that they chose to resume their football game. The boys eventually tired, kicked the ball hard against the fence and headed for their respective homes.

'When it emerged that the child was then reported missing, a major search was conducted in the local area. The house was gutted by local police, who reported that it had in fact been unoccupied for several months. In spite of their efforts, neither the boy nor Mrs Boden was ever found, though a bright red coat was spotted on a fence beside the crags upon the moorland.

'The house remained empty ever since; though if you ever go past at night, you might catch the soul-chilling, yearning wail of a bereft mother, or the cries of a young boy and the frantic rustling of long grass as he tries to escape his terrible fate.'

Fran and I were silent, though I sensed the stirring of the grey matter in her mind.

'So tell us why the boy disappeared. You have to tell us why. Did Mrs Boden kill him like she killed her own child? Or did she whisk him away to the crags so they could live happily together on the moorland, but she couldn't love him as much as her own child so she threw him down the-'

'How do you know she killed her own child?' Father asked.

'She did, everyone knows she did. I think she definitely did. You could tell because she didn't have any friends so she got depressed, and her husband didn't like her, probably because she always wore the same coat, and then one day she got so unhappy that she took it out on her child and she-'

'But do you think it possible that she could have-'

'Stop asking me. I want you to tell me, just make it up!'

'That's not like you, Fran.' In the yellow glow from the streetlight, I noticed a hopeless expression in Father's eyes;

they were like two peepholes in an empty dovecote. He reprised his observation, 'Not like you at all.'
'Can you tell us another story instead, then?' Fran asked.
'No.'
'Just make one up. Make one up about a grey lady who floats around in her tower and-'
'I'm trying to raise a pair of intelligent, thoughtful children here, Fran, and you're defying my efforts at every turn. Why don't we go back to the poem?'
'But we don't want to hear the poem; we want another story, an even scarier one, don't we?'
'Yes,' I said.
'Your little sister will be up all night, Fran.'
'She won't; she's not scared!'
I backed her, but my countenance, had it been daylight, would have suggested otherwise.
'If you keep pestering, young lady, then you won't hear another word out of me.'
'Fine. Then I hate you.' Fran ran on ahead, though her singing implied she had forgotten her indignation. I could hear crooning 'scary, scary, scary' as we approached the town centre. It was quiet. The air was stiff, gelatinous, and it promised thunder. Small buildings that were grey by day loomed black and tall. Those that were empty were surely emptier by night, I thought, or else occupied by beings of another kind. In spite of the heat, my hands were cold and clammy, and I realised as I got older that's how Father must have known I'd been afraid.

A week after school began again we were taken out of class to be told that our father had killed himself. He'd had about ten minutes to think better of it, but had died in the ambulance on the way to hospital. In a note destined for my mother, he'd mentioned an 'ugly carcinoma of irresolvable contradictions of character, among other things,' and for years I wondered if one of those other things could have been our refusal to listen to his poem.

## **Bottles**

Mr Narkissos turned the bottle over and over in his hand. It was a little small and nondescript for his taste, and he'd never liked cylindrical phials. Yet it was the olfactory notes that caught his attention:

Native to Turkey and Bulgaria and emboldened by aromas of Jasmine, Clover and Orange Blossom, the Damascus Rose provides the official note for this dark and alluring instance of alchemy. Created by Eric Andre Durand in 1996, the romantically-named Possession Cinq finds full expression on a dark winter's evening in the city, promising to transfix the senses amid glowing vapour lamps and satin sheets...

As his wife enjoyed reading the olfactory notes (and watching outtakes, and pouring over obituaries), Mr Narkissos was always obliged to choose a perfume worthy of its description. He noticed how she would roll the words over her tongue like an aniseed ball. Yet to him, the notes always sounded the same, and constituted an example of what he called 'made-up jobs for the mentally wimpled.' He did well, he thought, to appease what really was a most unusual hobby.

This was the first thing he joked about with his colleague Mr Peters, after reproaching him (jokingly, of course) for cutting things fine. Mr Peters was smaller than Mr Narkissos, who was only of medium height himself. They both wore blazers over bright white shirts; Mr Peters' was unbuttoned to reveal an eruption of grey chest hair which continued even to his crimson neck, while his colleague's was fastened by a tie across rough, turbid skin.

'Well, your Mary is certainly a one,' Mr Peters replied, placing down his suitcase and flexing his fingers.

'She certainly is,' said Mr Narkissos. 'Hey, it's a good job she's still got her uses, or happen I can think of plenty of young things in Sales who wouldn't say no to a bottle of Chanel; and

## The Tammersford Lot

I'd be surprised if they understood the olfactory notes, let alone made a bloody scrapbook out of them, or whatever the devil she does when I'm not there.' He held his colleague's arm and gave in to a burst of unmodulated laughter, each sound catching in his throat like the chug of an extractor fan. Only the roar of an incoming plane could drown him out. 'We haven't half been tempted over the years, have we, fellow? Eh, if you know what I mean.' Mr Narkissos dabbed at his brow with a napkin he had salvaged from his much below-par airport lunch.

'Oh, how we've been tempted.'

'I mean, it doesn't take a lot these days, does it, old boy?'

'Not a great deal these days, my friend.'

'You, you remember the Christmas do, with that girl with the, uh, the eyelashes…well, you know.'

'Well, I think a few of us slipped up that weekend, you know.'

'Well, quite.' Mr Narkissos regarded the perfume bottle in his hand. 'Quite.'

A loudspeaker announcement signalled that gate twelve A was now open. The men picked up their suitcases from the floor and Mr Narkissos proceeded to the checkout, telling his colleague he'd catch him in the waiting lounge.

At the announcement's close, he picked up on a jangle of chords in the mood music, and was instantly transported to an evening in London long ago. What had they seen (could it have been Les Miserables) when he and his wife had marvelled at the orange cocktails everybody was drinking, and the bar they visited had draped fairy lights about the rafters? That night, he had watched his wife strain to read the actor's profiles in the programme. He had watched her eat squid for the first time. As far as he could recall, they had forgotten to pay for two Irish coffees, and had ridden high on their fleeting status as white-collar criminals.

Another plane roared into earshot. The beautiful checkout girl assured Mr Narkissos that the accompanying shower gel was very good value for money, and he did not doubt her honesty. It would so happen that he refused it, and looked at the desk, mostly. She'd have no problem squeezing a bit of commission out of the next man, he thought (girls like that never did), so instead, he regarded the bottle for some time. He traced its cool edge, and twisted the lid to expose the scent. As the crowds filed past, he closed his eyes and breathed in Damascus Rose at length, lest it pall as he held it.

## **Selena and Edward**

Selena agreed to meet Edward at his house, because he'd told her he'd bought her a gift of sorts. His mother had recently bumped into her mother on the street, and the news that Edward still talked about Selena was enough to give her the courage to call him, say hello.

Besides, it wasn't just about Edward; his mother had been fond of Selena ever since they were both at primary school together, and there was something in that promise of approval that had spurred her on. And while her own mother had spent years worrying that their all being on friendly terms was born out of pity, Selena now had her job in the duty free shop. She was able to pay for tennis lessons and floaty tops. Last week, she'd treated herself to a ring: red cubic zirconia, set in silver.

Selena had spent the week going over what Edward had said on the phone, and it had made her morning walks to school all the happier. Past the silver birch trees, the empty bandstand, the shop with no window (still), then past the odd girl who walks in the morning, and at night, always the same way; as far as Selena's route was concerned, nothing had changed. The difference was in her: enlivened by a bright, crab apple sunrise, she would revisit the end of their conversation, which had begun as something of a tug-of-war between his dispirited interviewing and her attempts at coy indiscretion, and ended on a joyous note when she had told him her parents were going away at the weekend. She would delight in reliving the short pause that followed, imagining him cocking his head to one side, letting his long black hair fall over one eye as he had sweetly appropriated her old nickname and said, 'You should definitely come over to mine, then, Leeny. I know your mum used to be funny about stuff like that, so while the cat's away...I brought something back from my holiday, and I think you'd like it. So, you could come over, and I could give it to you.'

It was dark when Selena arrived, and was gradually beginning to rain (she was sure they were in for a winter of it, again). She held her jacket over her head, and was grateful for the warm air that had lingered from August because her arms were left bare. She'd managed to build up some muscle tone – the holidays had been dry enough for plenty of tennis practice – and she hoped Edward would notice. She rang the doorbell. A full moon floated in the Georgian porch glass.

'Selena, how nice to see you!' Edward's mother took her jacket and placed it on the hanger. 'Funny, I only saw your mother last Friday! What a nice surprise. Come in, come in, you'll get drenched, for heaven's sake.'

'Thank you.'

'Goodness, I don't think I've seen you for years! You're looking very well. So grown up. Had Edward mentioned that you were coming over, I would have offered for you to join us for supper, though I suspect they may be ordering a pizza in. Can I get you a drink of anything to take up?'

'Oh, no, I'm fine, thanks.' Selena paused. 'Sorry, who's ordering a pizza in?'

'He's got a few of his friends over. I know you're not in the sixth form yet, but you might recognise one or two of them. He's got his smartest shirt on, though, so I imagine it'll be you he's looking forward to seeing!'

Selena held her arms in her hands, feeling suddenly cold, empty; familiarly so, she noticed. She lingered, considering a retreat: it should be fast, silent, politely accounted for later. But Edward's mother smiled and wrinkled her nose, and that proved far too impassable a blockade to overcome. Selena found herself climbing the stairs, slowly, and following the sound of laughter to a room at the end of the landing.

## The Tammersford Lot

The door was half open. It only took a second's eavesdropping to tell her that both boys and girls were present. Tentatively, she nudged the door and peered inside.

'Leeny!' Edward was sat amid a small group of friends, his body relaxed and spread wide over a desk chair. Between his lips, an unlit cigarette flicked up and down, up and down. Selena noticed he was holding a large bottle of gin. Each clutching a plastic cup, it was unclear to her whether the guests were hanging on the promise of alcohol or Edward's every word. Either way, their being crouched on all fours at his feet reminded her of a pack of hyenas, waiting on the promise of a carcass.

'Leeny, hi.' Was that surprise or delight in his voice? 'Guys, this, this is Selena. She's from school, well she's not in our year, but I mean we've known each other for what? Ten years?'

Selena couldn't place his tone. She told him it was about that, yes, and seated herself – on Edward's offer – at the foot of the bed. The group swiftly repositioned itself to accommodate her, though between shuffles she thought she heard sighs.

'Gin?' Edward, who sat forward now, held out the bottle to her.

'Sure.'

A pretty girl with dark eyes and lips the colour of grenadine placed her fingers on Edward's shoulder. She leaned into him and whispered, 'Does babysitting pay by the hour, or do we get commission for feeding her?'

The comment was surely meant for Selena's ears. She cleared her throat, looked at the ceiling then inspected the contents of her bag. One side of Edward's mouth appeared to coil into a smirk, and the hyenas shuffled and sniggered through their teeth until the room was as sibilant as a hissing kettle.

'Ignore them, Leeny,' Edward said. Then he smiled fully, and she thought she caught a reflection of the moon in his eyes. 'We were just talking about the new principal. Darcy here had a run-in with him this afternoon. Apparently smoking in the sixth form grounds isn't allowed anymore.' The pretty girl raised an eyebrow and motioned for Edward to pass her the gin. 'He's a nice guy, don't get me wrong, but he's clearly out of his depth, isn't he?' he continued. 'He's just tinkering with things, trying to make an impact. It's like he's too afraid to really go for it, you know?' The hyenas lapped up Edward's words, their tongues dangling like flatworms. 'We're just going to have to watch our backs. You'll be alright, Leeny, you're just a sprite.' He added, 'Have you ever even smoked?'

'Yes, well, I've tried it. I've tried it loads of times, actually. I mean, I like it. I like it, but I might have a bit of a cough coming on, so...'

'Probably overdoing it with those cigarettes.'

Edward took the gin back from Darcy; Selena thought she saw him wink by way of a thank you. She stayed silent, but there were only so many times she could look at the ceiling and down at her bag without somebody calling her out on it.

Edward, on the other hand, was almost cruelly at ease. He barely had to toy with his cigarette before Darcy produced a light. Her eyes on Selena, she placed it between her grenadine lips and lit it for him.

'Do you know what I remember about you, Leeny?' Edward continued. 'You were the prettiest little girl in town. You used to jog past my old house – remember, the four story one up towards the moorland – and I thought to myself, that is, I mean that is...the prettiest girl in town. I mean, she is going to break her share of hearts, I thought.'

Selena smiled modestly, and thanked him. It was a warm smile that came from years of longing and imagining, and when he returned it she felt her life's pastime vindicated. But she also felt Darcy's dark eyes. Like the cautionary drone of two black bees, she was finding them ever harder to ignore.

'This town's pretty small,' Darcy said. She cast her head towards her friends and laughed through her nose. They reciprocated. Edward drew breath, mockingly.

'It won't be small for long,' he went on, 'not once they get rid of that forest and start building. And if they did away with

## The Tammersford Lot

some of the older neighbourhoods – you know, the ones with houses that look like shacks down by the bandstand – there'd be far more scope to extend the town.' Edward paused to take a drag. He held his cigarette between four fingers, as if he were blowing a poisoned dart. 'Sorry, Leeny, I mean, sorry, where do you guys live these days?'

'Oh, we're, we're just, we're going to sell up, soon. My parents are looking to buy maybe a couple of properties in town.' She flicked her hands forward as she spoke, perhaps to extract the lie by force, or perhaps to insist they invest in it. 'Been saving for a while.'

'A couple, eh?' Darcy's eyes widened. Her voice was suddenly gruff, 'How t'other 'alf live.'

'You know, I reckon I'm probably just going to head off,' Selena said, surprising even herself. 'I think I'm getting this cough thing and I'm just pretty shattered, to be honest. But it was nice to meet you all. I hope you have a good night.'

'Leeny, don't go, are you mad?' Edward stood up, shaking Darcy loose. 'We were just going to order food. I mean, are you sure?'

'Yeah honestly, I'm just tired.'

'Well, I mean, if you're sure.'

'I'm sure. I'll see you around.'

She left quickly. The landing was dark and drafty and far cooler than Edward's room. She crept down the stairs, hoping not to run into his mother. Slipping her shoes on and reclaiming her jacket, she slid into the night, buffeted by an onslaught of rain.

'Selena!'

Half way down the drive, she turned to see Edward running towards her. The rain quickly reduced his crisp shirt to a limp casing, like paper soaked in grease.

'I'm sorry about tonight. Didn't organise myself very well, did I?'

'It's fine.'

'Really?'

'Yeah. I'm just going to go home and watch the telly, or something. Rest up, you know.'

'Oh, well. It's just, I mean, I brought you something, remember? But here, we'll need to stand under this tree, come.'

He steered Selena under an oak tree and moved in close to her. Glancing behind him, he opened his hand.

'What is it?' Selena asked.

'Here, take him, he's yours. But be really careful; I think he's at death's door. Go on, turn him over.'

Selena held the gift in her hand and rolled him over with the tip of her finger. The three bars of green light on the creature's tail told her it must have been a firefly.

'Like emeralds,' Edward whispered.

'Where did you get this?'

'I told you, I brought him home from my holiday. I thought you might like him. God knows how he survived the journey back. He must have sensed he'd eventually go to a good home.' He wiped a spray of rain from Selena's cheek. 'Well, do you like him?'

Selena looked at Edward. The vitreous moon languished in his hair and eyes, and she vowed in that moment that had she the means and the skill, she would like to have him sleep beside her forever, unfettered in form, and far from the cloying advances of others. In that instant, she resolved to unlearn all that her instinct had told her about Edward, and would invest fully in the version of him he presented before her now. Certainly, she had been flat wrong about him, all those years. Why ever had she been so guarded?

'I love him.'

'Now why don't you come back with me later, Leeny? This little guy can light our walk home. And surely if he can survive a flight and all, I mean we should honour that, you and me. We'll go into town and get a few drinks at the Social – they'll serve me, my dad pays everyone's wages there – then we could head back to mine, by which time my parents should have gone to bed.'

'Well, I mean…well, what about your friends?'

'Give me fifteen minutes to get rid of them. Meet me in the town centre, next to Community Lodge, ok? We can walk to yours from there. You look beautiful tonight, Leeny.' He leaned into her as he said it, leading with his cheek rather than his lips; Selena thought, their proximity was too ambiguous to merit her attempting to kiss them.

She said, 'I'll meet you there. I'll go there now, ok?'

She forgot about the rain. She let her jacket hang loose about her shoulders and held the firefly close, pausing every few minutes to check it hadn't fallen out of her hands. When she reached Community Lodge, she positioned herself beneath the open porch. The old wooden door smelled damp and earthy. The firefly twitched; only two bars on its tail now glowed.

After an hour, there remained only one bar. The rain had doused the silver birch trees until they shone in the moonlight; beyond them, Selena noticed the odd girl who walks in the morning, and at night – always the same route. The girl had the familiar look this evening, strained, like hypertension, pushing out against the tubular rain. Selena bent down. The wet stone was cold against her knees. Gently, she placed the firefly under a loose shard of slate, for she recalled how she'd once hit a bee with her tennis racket and it had slowly proceeded to bury itself, as though seeing to a final act of preordained dignity that merited a far worthier witness than she.

## The Rowan Tree

The first memory I planned to recount would take us back twenty years. With his father's dismal collusion, a then eight-year old Craig had brought a gobstopper to the neighbourhood's Conkering Championships, persuading every parent present (let's not forget that fetching smile and the twinkly blue eyes) of his intentions: he'd decimate his opponent's weapon and create a lasting reminder of how damaging sweets could be to one's teeth.

There is a story – potentially apocryphal – that upon hearing Craig's idea, the corner shop lady gave him the gobstopper for free, no doubt wanting to find favour with the neighbourhood's most insouciantly radical child.

Sadly, Craig had lost in the quarter finals to twin brother Colum, his equal in stature and strength yet already a strong contender for the title. For the seven months that followed, Colum had displayed his conker on their bedroom windowsill, refusing to remove this fast-putrefying symbol of fraternal defeat until Aunty Wendy went at it with a glass and a postcard, just as one might get rid of a wasp or large spider.

I could still remember the stench it left, and how it filled your nostrils not on every inhalation; rather, when somebody's movement incurred a small draft, or when you reached up to the shelf to take a board game. I remembered how it turned from mahogany to indigo-black with fierce bubbles of white. When we'd visit (which was almost every day at one point), I'd always insist that we check on the conker, and would gleefully point out how it was starting to resemble the head of a warty turbot. Surprisingly, Craig had been most discomfited by its removal; having quickly reconciled himself to Colum's having the brawn, he formed an identity around possession of the brains, and did not once lament that their identical build had not afforded him as much athletic prowess. He delighted in the conker's vile demise and was able to forget what it had represented, and it was only after many years that I came to admire such a swift and radical acceptance of self.

As I polished the wine glasses, I thought about recounting this story as soon as I'd poured everyone a drink. Or perhaps I'd tell it once we were seated at the table. Yes. Initial small talk would address the present, the starter could take care of the past, and the main course would lend itself naturally to talk of the future. I'd chew stoically, take a sip of wine, and wait for the right moment to make my announcement (this would also give me enough time to watch how Craig's fiancé conducted herself and do likewise. I had toyed with the idea of taming my hair, parting it down the middle and wearing it loose like hers, but her face was a perfect heart and mine too narrow; they might have said I looked a little harsh).

Of course, it was always what she did as opposed to what she said that interested me; the first time I met Leah, about three years ago, now, she drank two glasses of wine and fell into graceful taciturnity, like a marshmallow sinking into hot cocoa.

We'd been Christmas tree hunting in Mason's Forest (in the awkward part that jutted almost into the centre of town as opposed to the forest proper). The weather had been cold and enfeebling, and I could see Leah falling asleep on the train ride home. Portent or miracle, the snow that had begun in November that year had lingered for a good two weeks or more, yet the fresh Pyrenean air – a most welcome accompaniment to the surprise flurry – did not last. I remembered how Craig had supported her dollish head the entire journey, and how he'd carried her to the car like a newborn lamb. I'd tried to focus on the scene below; the shelterbelts around the fields, the huge chimneys, the old mill and its confusing outdoor fitments – copper ingots and tyres – and finally the Christmas crowds as we neared the town centre, pushing and shoving with veteran aplomb. But the delicacy of those interactions had clung to me like filet lace, and I became most aware of a desire to run, or plunge head first into a hot bath.

The table was set for dinner so I circled it twice to check that nothing was missing. Uncle Andrew would sit at the head of the table – as had always been customary at get-togethers – while Aunty Wendy would sit to his right and to her right would be Colum, then Leah. Grandmother would sit opposite Uncle Andrew (her sherry glass was already in place), I would sit to her right, and then Craig would sit next to me. The spare place next to Craig would be used as a collection and drop-off point, meaning there would be ample space for the pre-warmed plates, for example. I placed tall items such as the carafe on Uncle Andrew's side, so whether Leah was silent or not, I could observe and copy her uninhibited. 'You're not as you once were, Joanna,' they might say.

Such posturing would surely fuel an image of an altogether sunnier person. I lit the tea lights on the mantelpiece and hid the empty shoe rack behind the sofa. With an hour before their arrival, I still had time to display my paintings, dedicate a good twenty minutes (possibly twenty-five) for practising Dutch, and – being slightly ahead of schedule – I could even squeeze in my evening walk (taking care to venture only as near to the forest as would permit a little fresh air; I didn't really want to run into anybody for fear of having to make small talk). An influx of new projects necessitated a stricter routine, these days, and I was anxious not to let it elude me.

I sat on the kitchen windowsill watching the light fade outside. The yellowy fog that clabbered above the hills began to taper as it reached Mason's Forest, sending a trill of gurning shadows across the window pane. When a sudden burst of streetlamp light revealed my reflection and roused me to fresh appraisals of my appearance, I decided a much better attempt at make-up was warranted. Not for the first time, the liminal instant between day and night had found me somewhere between self-loathing and an unfair yet unshakeable annoyance at others; I was a human fulcrum upon which seesawed a feeling of general disdain. I pulled my grammar notes toward me and opted to revisit the future tense.

– 'I will go; ik zal gaan.'
– 'You will go; jij zult gaan.'

It suddenly occurred to me that the guests might like an amuse-bouche before the starter. I began to panic; we'd never bothered with such things in the past, but Leah and Craig frequently held dinner parties and I wondered if that was the kind of thing they were used to.

– She will go; zij zal gaan.
– He will go; hij zal gaan.

I could have put a few crisps out but I knew they'd only ask for dip. The salsa I had would leave a residual taste such that might detract from the flavour of the starter.

– I will not go; ik zal niet gaan.

What if they discovered my grammar notes? There were too many assumptions to be made about my motives, each of which had to be imparted in a timely manner in such a way as to obviate any semblance of the arbitrary. My decision was no whim. In truth, I had come to loathe this language (there were far too many Ks than I was used to, straight and stern like split wood down the page), but it was a necessary precursor to the level of conviction with which I'd deliver my news. I was about to pull the curtain to when a knock at the door took me by surprise.

It was five thirty. It couldn't be them. They'd surely arrive late and leave early? I retrieved my paintings, placed them hurriedly around the living room and threw on a smart jacket.

'Hello, how's it going? Everyone alright?' I stood to the side to let Uncle Andrew through. Colum and Aunty Wendy followed; their hair carried a layer of water droplets. 'You're very early.' My voice was hardly nonchalant.

'Your hair looks darker; almost black, in fact,' said Grandmother, easing her slow, distended body through the door. 'Don't forget to condition it with every wash.' I went to kiss her but, with intent or not, she sidestepped me like a puddle.

'Throw your coats on the sofa and do help yourselves to a drink. I have wine in the fridge and there's some gin and sherry on the cabinet.'

I followed Colum and Aunty Wendy into the living room. Wendy poured them each a gin, complimented my canvasses and asked how long I'd been painting for.

'Maybe a year or so,' I said. 'I did most of these last spring. Isn't it a shame that the bluebells always disappear so fast?'

Aunty Wendy agreed. 'So how are you, Jo? Such a nice idea, to get us all together. I'm sorry it's been so long, I mean I suppose, well, you let life get on top of you, don't you? Always things to be done!'

'Always! No, I'm fine, absolutely fine. Shame about this horrible weather, though, isn't it? Is it very foggy out?' I already knew the answer, of course.

Uncle Andrew crouched in the doorway, loosening the laces on his boots. He accepted a gin and paused briefly to take a sip. In the dim light of the hallway he looked a lot older than I remembered.

'Considerably,' he replied. 'It made the journey rather difficult. And then Grandmother took a while to get going, of course.'

Aunty Wendy clapped her hands, and continued, 'So we were trying to work out how long it had actually been since we last saw each other. Andrew thought it might have been over a year, because we didn't see you last Christmas in the end, did we, what with Leah's family asking us round? Craig and Leah are on their way. I think they stopped off to buy some beers.'

I nodded and smiled. Remembering that Leah, once seen, creates a vision that defies temporal boundaries, and that her comportment can rouse within you the sense of being fully formed and wholly terrestrial while part of you – the part that never learned to be – floats frozen, exanimate and goading, just out of range, I felt myself empty like a tumbler. I recalled her long fair hair and the beechnut mole on her cheek.

'My pleasure,' I said. 'I suppose it's just, you know; if you don't make the effort-'

'Yes, yes, well exactly,' said Aunty Wendy. 'You haven't been slaving away all day, then, have you?'

'The meal didn't take too long to prepare, and I could have spent longer on the tidying.' I poured Grandmother a small sherry.

'Here you are, Grandmother. It's lovely to have you over. Aunty Wendy was just saying the last time we all saw each other must have been over a year ago.'

'Thank you. It was last Christmas and you filled a plate with mud from the garden, which I suppose you thought was very funny.'

In the silence that followed, I cast a nervous glance at Uncle Andrew, who shook his head slightly.

'I think that was a good twenty years ago,' I told her gently. 'And besides, the twins and I, we did that together. Christmas mud pies with a layer of snow instead of cream!'

'Bit early for Christmas talk, isn't it?' Craig announced his entrance loudly – and who would have expected anything less? He held a bag of beers in each hand.

'Well, I imagine it was your idea,' Grandmother said. 'You always took an interest in the queerest of games. Odd that you had to implicate the twins to further your own daft ends.'

I stepped back as Grandmother made to embrace Craig, who held her arm as he kissed her and when she spoke, he nodded intently. I looked at Uncle Andrew again; his eyes wandered to the ceiling, the drinks cabinet, the floor. Colum, on the other hand, actively sought my gaze – but when our eyes met I was immediately distracted by how dissimilar he and his brother had become.

Craig was slim and straight backed. He wore pointy shoes and lapels. His dark waves had become so precise that they were nearly angular, and ran like a circuit of droveways almost over his ears, indicating his sideburns and strong jaw. Beneath his dark eyebrows flashed those blue eyes, darker now, like delftware, set between a nest of black lashes that seemed to multiply as you watched. Colum's posture was stooped, his hair unruly; his brow twitched and, sometimes, his neck with it.

'Hello, cousin,' Craig suddenly leaned into me, then withdrew and held an arm out to Leah. 'You remember my lovely fiancée, don't you?' When he had removed his coat he helped her remove hers.

'Yes of course,' I said, and kissed her once on the cheek. 'Congratulations on the engagement.'

'Thank you, and thank you for having us,' she said. Her face was lightly powdered and she'd swept half her hair into a neat bouffant; she reminded me of a calla lily.

'You're most welcome. What can I get you to drink, Leah?'

'Oh, I'm fine,' she said.

'Are you sure? There's a bottle of wine in the fridge if you're not keen on spirits. Would you like me to make you a spritzer?'

'Yes, ok, just a small spritzer. Thank you. And a water, please.'

'Don't force the poor lamb if she doesn't want a drink,' said Grandmother. 'She's entitled to refuse a drink before a meal. When Sally Morag had us round for supper there was no talk of drink before a meal, only during; or after. There was Sally and Christopher, and poor Peggy Byrne who lost her young husband. She never was the same without him. She used to wet her hair and pat it down flat so it stuck to her head, and when it dried she'd go to the bathroom and wet it again. Now isn't that a strange thing to do?'

Leah nodded, and turned to look at Craig.

'Well no one knows, do they, what loss can drive you to?' he said, and returned her gaze as he brought a beer to his lips.

Grandmother placed a finger on her mouth and frowned slightly. 'It is rather chilly,' she announced finally. 'Colum, take a match from my handbag and see to it that the gas is turned on.' She watched as he struggled with the control knob.

'It looks dreadfully stiff to turn. Surely you must have used it recently, Joanna?'

'I don't bother with it much; in fact I don't think it's been used since last winter. You need brute force to twist it.' I clambered down beside Colum and had him hold the match while I turned on the gas.

'Let him turn it,' barked Grandmother. 'You see to it that everyone that wants one has a drink in their hand.'

I asked feebly if everyone was ok for drinks and suggested they topped themselves up when they were ready, indicating the bottles on the newly-polished cabinet.

'Thank you, Jo,' said Aunty Wendy. There was a short pause.

'It's going to rain, again,' Uncle Andrew said. 'It's been a mighty odd year for weather. Can't say I've enjoyed it one bit.'

'Oh it's been bloody horrendous,' Craig replied. 'I'd slay a few folk just to see a bit of snow this Christmas, but I doubt it's going to happen. Look at last year. Bloody wash out, it was.'

'I fully agree,' I said. 'If only–'

'You mustn't frown so, Joanna,' Grandmother barked. She opened her mouth again as if to continue, but instead turned her attention to the dinner table. 'Now, soup bowls. I suspect the boys were hoping for something a little more robust.'

'The soup's only a starter, Grandmother. I've prepared a nice stew for the main. Excuse me; I'll just fetch Leah's drink.'

I went into the kitchen and poured myself a large wine. I breathed in slowly, looking at the street outside. I was contemplating whether or not to prepare that spritzer when I noticed Colum had followed me in. He tugged at his collar vigorously.

'Alright, Colum? Can I get you anything?'

He indicated his gin. 'Just ice.'

'The journey was ok then, was it?' I asked, rummaging in the freezer.

'Oh yes, fine. Things alright with you?'

'Yes, fine thanks.' I realised I didn't have any ice cubes so proceeded to chisel away at the frost in the drawers.

'I'll do that,' he said. 'Do you remember when we were little and you told me and Craig to bring you all the icicles we could find? You said if we melted them down and drank them they would bring us magic powers.'

'Yes, I do remember,' I laughed. 'Craig was so keen to fill the bucket I think he checked every windowsill in the neighbourhood!'

Colum dropped what ice he had managed to remove into his glass and raised it up.

'Cheers,' he said. 'To magic.'

'To magic.'

When he had left the room I took a sip of wine and turned back to the window. The fog seemed to remain over the hills and the outermost part of the forest and for once looked like it might not descend into the town. Colum's anecdote had stirred in me a sentiment so effaced from any present reality that I struggled to name it; like the first kick of a foetus, it was unexpected, subtle, and by warrant of Colum's rare joviality, a game changer. Gazing across the street, I saw Mrs Holmes draw her bathroom curtains. The announcement I had planned seemed suddenly churlish.

'I'm afraid I don't actually have any soda water, Leah,' I called. 'Would you like just a small glass of wine?' She refused the offer with tonal cordiality, and I was glad that she didn't come into the kitchen.

'Sorry to leave you,' I said as I re-entered the living room. They had formed a small circle with a point of entry; I felt like an actor in an amphitheatre. No doubt their most recent memories of me comprised a sour face and a series of tendentious assertions, offered solely as a means to contradict whatever viewpoint they held and channel the spirit of my then-boyfriend, a subversive professor who shaped my thoughts for half a year. The recollection of my conduct was a cause of acute embarrassment to me, and I hoped to put things right tonight. I remembered how Craig and Uncle Andrew seemed to sneer whenever I started to speak, and the distance that had slowly taken form between us over the years seemed hopelessly unalterable. Still, at least this period had served to erase the memory of my unacceptable teenage years; chiding me for my unrealised plans to live in a tent outdoors was a habit to which Grandmother no longer had recourse.

'Everyone ok for drinks, then?'

'Yes, thank you, Jo,' said Aunty Wendy. 'Now I noticed your Dutch book on the windowsill - wasn't it French you were learning last time we saw you?'

Oh French. I immediately missed those evening classes, laughing and waving flash cards; discovering familiar dark vowels, like soft, black cherries in a compote of otherwise difficult sounds that stuck in the glottis. That, and the concept of mountains.

'Well, Dutch is just an extra, I suppose; it's just something I'm dabbling in.' They would know more later. 'I'm enjoying it, I mean I look forward to practising it, so I take that as a positive sign, I mean I don't know what it'll lead to yet, but there you are. How is the card business?'

'Good, thank you. In fact Leah submitted some of her drawings for our Christmas range - they've proven very popular with our clients.'

'Oh how very lovely,' said Grandmother. 'Tell me, dear, do you still teach art?'

'Leah's a teaching assistant, Grandmother,' said Craig. 'But she taught her first lesson the other day because the teacher was off sick.'

'I was asked at the last minute. Mrs Abbott asked me to do a lesson on water colours, though I was worried that the children might be too young to master the technique. I brought in some beautiful geraniums from the garden, and we tried to paint those,' Leah added.

'Now I very much enjoyed that afternoon in your new garden this summer,' said Grandmother. 'As I recall, there were fuchsias, and roses, and a big tall pear tree like the one that I had all those years ago.' Grandmother put her sherry to her lips, and continued, 'Andrew's father saw to it that, come spring time, we were never short of seeds and bulbs. He was very good like that, you see.'

'Hear, hear,' said Craig. 'Did you know I'd taken on Colum as a draftsman, Grandmother?' He continued. 'I'm training him up. Even got him to wear a shirt. It's mostly ground coverings he's working on, but once he's fully confident with the calculations he can pitch to potential investors. I'm hoping to expand the company – maybe make a few connections abroad – so he'll really get a handle on service development as well.'

'How marvellous,' said Grandmother. 'And do people ever get you two confused?'

'Well Craig's the landscape designer - everyone knows he's the boss,' said Colum.

Craig laughed. 'Colum works hard. He knows the land. And not only can he shift things about, but he's sharp as well; it's not easy going from digging to drafting in one fell swoop. He got talked down at first, as can happen, and I mean he lost his temper a bit. We welcome that – nobody likes a pushover – but I told him he's got to hone his skills first. And he's pulled it back, you know. He really has. Comes in, calculates, sketches, eats, sketches, calculates. I mean there have been a few incidents, like the one with the drinks kitty, which we won't dwell on here. I mean it really doesn't pay to dwell on mistakes, does it? I'm sure if he'd carried on with that gardening job any longer he'd have looked like Quasimodo, though he has had to do the odd lifting job because of this...' he reached behind him and rubbed the skin behind his left ear and continued, '...bloody crick in my neck that won't shift.'

'My serfdom has been duly vanquished,' said Colum.

Craig laughed again, and said: 'All that's left to do now is to find you a woman. When you find her, confine yourself to her.' He hugged Leah close, and laughed again.

## The Tammersford Lot

The soup had been warming for a good hour, and I was suddenly aware of its smell. I was relieved when Uncle Andrew asked when we were eating.

'The soup's ready when we are,' I said. 'Take a seat and I'll serve it out.'

A month ago I was on my evening walk through Mason's Forest. I contoured along the edge, keeping to the path, as usual, and there was an unearthly stillness, the trees roused only by the occasional light wind. From higher ground, I could see how the linear flow of trees had been interrupted by the odd patch of wasteland, where some trees had been felled. I took a moment to taste the damp air, and was at once dually startled by a salvo of discordant bird calls – a triumphant, self-assured chorus – and an enormous rowan tree to my right. Its branches were ablaze and ready for autumn, and I could have gone left or right but decided to linger for a moment, wishing we could go there, all of us together. We could climb it, Craig and Colum and I, and call back towards Aunty Wendy's camera; they may remark that I looked like my mother when I smiled. I would crush the orange berries and rub them against Craig's neck to make him itch. Or was that rosehips?

Perhaps that was rosehips, I thought as I ladled the soup into bowls. Rowan berries never made anybody itch, unless they were allergic to them. I offered the basket of bread rolls and told everyone to tuck in.

'This looks very nice,' said Aunty Wendy. 'Tomato?'

'And basil,' I replied.

'And what did you use to thicken the soup?' asked Craig, sampling it.

'Just a little corn flour,' I replied.

'Yes, I thought so.' He abandoned his spoon – smiling slightly – and reached for the butter knife, which he used to sever a bread roll in two.

'Why do you ask, Craig? Surely you can't taste it?' Carelessly I managed to sound more accusatory than I'd intended. I observed Leah to regain composure; she ate delicately and dabbed at her mouth with a napkin.

'It was just a hunch,' said Craig.

'We thought we saw a deer on the way here,' said Aunty Wendy. I noticed she too had set down her spoon. 'We saw a big pair of eyes peeping out from between the bushes, but he disappeared as we got close. He was probably spooked by the headlights, poor bean.'

'I wish I'd seen it,' I said. 'I once had about twenty run right passed me in the woods. They would have trampled me had I been in their path. I felt lucky to be alive, so I tried to make the event meaningful, but the most I could do was look up the word 'deer' in French and recount the event to my classmates-'

'And I suppose they encourage narcissistic ramblings about oneself and one's achievements in these classes?' Grandmother's voice was high and tinny.

I explained, 'We're actually encouraged to describe and discuss a range of perspectives, Grandmother, and-'

'There are lumps in this soup!' She cried suddenly. 'Doughy little lumps. Whatever are you feeding us, Joanna?'

My heart sank as Craig began to tut mockingly.

'I'm sorry, everybody, it must be the corn flour. I can't have stirred it in properly. Really, I'm sorry. Hopefully the main will be better.' I stood up to collect their bowls but Craig held his hand up.

'Just leave them for now, Jo; Colum's enjoying it,' he said. Bowl in hand, Colum was rapidly spooning the soup into his mouth; in these disordered movements his gracelessness showed. His lips were red and his hair even curlier with the steam. I sat back down, though out of embarrassment he signalled for me to remove the bowl.

'Well, these things happen,' said Uncle Andrew. 'What kind of stew have you prepared?'

'Lamb,' I said. 'I just have to quickly make the mint sauce. Excuse me.'

I gathered the bowls in rounds and insisted that no one help. Once in the kitchen, I dimmed the light and stared outside. To my surprise, the fog suddenly lay much closer now, curled about the houses, yellowy and immotile. I pushed half a bread roll into my stomach and took a gulp of wine.

Somewhat tormented by nerves, I questioned the purpose of my announcement; I'd been strategising for months, and had finally settled on a plan so fail-safe that would surely render their seeing me as more than a simple obligation. I would be of interest to them, doing the things they approved of and all; I would be transformed (tonight was a mere prelude, the final shreds of the pupa before full eclosion) and ready to enter their world fully, without the need for offerings. I prepared to relay the conker story, the account I'd hoped would be an appropriate lead-in.

Talk had turned to cooking as I placed the stew and mint sauce on the table. I'd forgotten to warm the plates, so Aunty Wendy offered to do it as I fetched the potatoes.

'When it comes to stewing steak,' Craig said as I placed them in the centre of the table, 'you've got to find the right butcher. Now good stewing steak is cut from the skirt, chuck, leg or flank – the muscles that work hard – and they need to be cooked slowly or they'll go all chewy. If you go to a butcher, he'll cut the chunks far larger than you'll get in a supermarket, so there's something to really get your teeth into.

'Leah and I have a routine, don't we, darling?' He surveyed us to make sure he had our attention. 'Wednesday evening, Leah will bring back a nice big bit of stewing steak.' He indicated the size with his hands. 'I'll buy us a bottle of red – we try something new every week, don't we? – And we'll drink a few glasses with the meal. In goes a bit of stock, couple of onions, carrots, what have you, into the oven, then about half way through I'll remind Leah to put the potatoes on and she'll have them peeled, boiled and mashed by the time the stew's ready. We're thinking of having our kitchen done out so there'll be more space. We want it to be the centre of the home, you know? Breakfast bar, a bit of pop art on the walls, maybe a stove-top coffee maker.'

I handed him a plate of stew and he helped himself to some potatoes. He went on:

'And the key to a great stew? A bit of sea salt cracked over the top, and just a few sprigs of fresh rosemary – see these bits of lamb are smaller than we're used to, aren't they, Leah? – And you know you can get exactly the same amount of meat from a butcher, but he'll slice it thicker. And Jo, it helps if you bat your eyes a little when he's carving - you might wind up with a bit extra.'

He looked over at Leah. She smiled shyly, blushing somewhat, and a sudden conviction in the plans I intended to share rose within me as the wine surged to my head. I filled the last plate and sat up straight, chin raised, wrists resting on the table's edge, ready.

'With poise and grace, a woman can achieve anything,' Grandmother suddenly squalled through a mouthful of stew. 'A slow, lolloping gait and a sour puss will make a man run a mile, as will a short temper. Your mother had a fiery temper too, Joanna, right up to her final days, I don't know if you'll remember.' She drank a little sherry and sat back slightly in her chair. 'Now when we used to play Postman's Knock, just before the war, the girls that knew how to conduct themselves well were the ones the boys wanted to kiss the most. Mark me here. I always made sure to wear heels and a smart coat, and Jonny Hutton only ever had eyes for me.'

'What's Postman's Knock?' asked Craig.

'Oh it was ever such a lot of fun,' Grandmother replied. 'Colum, take some of my meat, it's too tough for my jaw. The girls would sit around a room and the boys would assemble in another. Then one would come and knock at the door with a letter, and each girl would take it in turns to answer the door and pay for it with a kiss. When it was my turn, and it was

Jonny at the door, well, it sent my head spinning. But I'd have led a sorry life with him; all he ever wanted to do was join the air force, and lo and behold, soon as the war broke out, he did. But your Grandfather was a very good man; he was a hard worker and a high earner, and he sacrificed a lot to keep us in that house, the four of us. And never once did I let standards slip, not even when things got tough. The home, the garden; spotless, everything spotless, and two children raised very well indeed. And I was always smartly turned out and well mannered.'

'Except when you threw his clothes into the street when he slept in a ditch after a night at the pub.' I expected a laugh, but my assertion had left a contrail of discomfort. Leah glanced up and blinked and I immediately felt embarrassed. I'd done this before, present a roster of home truths, and they'd remember, of course, because it was at Mum's funeral. And the time afterwards, two years ago, which they were less forgiving of given the absence of raw grief. Outside, the fog had given way to rain, as was usual for this time of the evening, and I noticed Uncle Andrew turn and stare as each drop detonated against the windowpane.

'I can assure you that I did nothing of the sort.' Grandmother put down her cutlery and pointed a finger at me. 'You always were one for stories, Joanna, and I'd urge you to take caution when implicating others in these wild ideas.'

'Mother-' Uncle Andrew interjected.

'I take exception to that remark, Grandmother, and I'm damn tired of always having to-'

'That's quite enough, now.' Aunty Wendy shot me a look that made my nerves jangle. I was on my feet, leaning over Grandmother. Everybody was silent. Uncle Andrew looked hopelessly from the window to the floor.

'I'm sorry. Don't know what came over me, I...'

I took my seat again, slowly, and continued to eat in silence. The conversation careened desperately from Aunty Wendy's card business to organic vegetables to taxes, and when all the cutlery had been set in a cross over each plate (the potatoes had mostly been eaten; the meat was toyed with at best), I began to clear.

'Take it easy on your Grandmother, Jo. She's...struggling.' Aunty Wendy had followed me into the kitchen.

'Yes, I see that. I mean I didn't know it had got so...but really, I assure you, I mean I haven't been living here long and these walls have never seen the side of me that she brings out. And that time, two years ago, you know, when I, when I threw that plate at the wall...I mean, she provoked me, she shouldn't have said-'

'Well, come on now, let's not dwell on things,' said Aunty Wendy. 'You know what she can get like. Now I say we wait a while before pudding, don't you? I think we'd all benefit from a little sherry and a stretch out in the living room.'

'It's just that-'

'Now, now. Let's get this lot cleared up then we can all relax.'

She moved swiftly, barely leaving a streak as she scraped the contents of each plate into the bin. She was smaller these days; her shoulders were hunched and her head bowed forward, though her dexterity belied her age and posture. I noticed she had fallen into a pattern – scrape, rinse, stack – and was able to execute her task with all the flow of an organ player mid piece. I tried to work around her but ended up just tinkering with the cutlery.

'I'll invite them back through to the living room,' I said. Aunty Wendy nodded, apparently concentrating. I touched her arm and thanked her, lingering for a moment before leaving the kitchen.

When I returned to the table, Grandmother was talking to Leah, inquiring about her hair, possibly, and Craig was discussing work. I poured myself some more wine and sat in Aunty Wendy's place to listen.

'See he, he wants to build a helter-skelter there,' said Craig, pointing at his brother. 'I told him it wouldn't last a day. Local yobbos would trash it within hours. Seconds. First thing they'd do, they'd take their penknives to the paint work.' He took a gulp of wine, winced, and continued, 'Thing is, and I shouldn't really be saying this, but my company's been given a small commission to tarmac over a couple of the fields just before the moorland. I mean again, keep this to yourself, but we're party to all sorts of plans the council's toying with at the moment,' Craig continued. 'What I'm saying is, they want car parks, children's parks, complexes. These moves are going to bring a real beating heart to Tammersford. I'm not exaggerating; this town has got the potential – I mean, spatial and otherwise – to really thrive; even with all this bloody rain! And I mean, we'll be...' Craig lowered his voice and leaned in towards Uncle Andrew, '...I mean we'll be singing all the way to the bloody bank when it comes off, you know? Leah and I could finally afford a detached place. I mean you could probably afford somewhere with its own garden, Colum, and you could even get a little motor so you wouldn't have to walk everywhere, especially when it pours down.'

'Then I would miss things. I'd miss the sounds you get, like the sound of the rain.' Colum failed to lift his gaze from his glass. Craig seemed to be forging their path as we spoke but such never used to be the law of Colum's being; nonetheless, they both appeared bound to a most inevitable conclusion the realisation of which my announcement would perhaps bear no impact.

Uncle Andrew asked about pudding just as Aunty Wendy came back into the room. She suggested that everyone retire to the sofas, so I went to pour another glass of wine and told them I would follow them through; turning off the hallway light, I watched Craig go immediately to Leah, as though their being at separate ends of the table were a source of great discomfort to him. The two of them regarded my paintings, and in the flickering candle light I saw him place his hand on the small of her back. I couldn't be sure, but he seemed amused by something; and she laughed when he did.

Outside, the rain continued to pour. Grandmother was dozing by the fireside; Leah and the twins were watching television with the sound down. Leah didn't use the back rest on the couch so neither did I; we all said little. Colum was working on his trifle in a most peculiar way: pushing it down and outwards so it met the rim of the bowl, he proceeded to carve a pyramid of sorts, devouring most of the sponge, custard and cream but leaving a stoic base of jelly and fruit, with only a narrow peak left in the middle to account for the other layers. Working his way in a circle from the outside in, once he perfected his shape he left what remained in the bowl, clearly finding the lowermost layers a less than agreeable source of palliation. When he finished, he placed the bowl on the floor and looked about him nervously, as though suddenly conscious of the fact that he was in a room with others.

Uncle Andrew, who had been listening to Aunty Wendy whisper at length about Grandmother's faltering memory and his unusually excessive consumption of gin, prolonged his response with palpable effort, then asked suddenly: 'The bay window in your kitchen, Jo – does it open? I'd like to breathe a little fresh air.'

'Yes it does. You really need to force it, though and…I'll just show you,' I replied, and he followed me into the kitchen.

'I often sit here with the lights off at night,' I said, indicating the large windowsill. I heaved the window up until it was open two or three inches. Uncle Andrew lowered his head to the opening and appeared to breathe in deeply and at length, as though willing the air to quench a great and indefatigable thirst.

I tried again: 'Would you like me to turn off the lights? Dim them?'

'Dim them,' he said eventually, not taking his eyes off the rain. I did so, and was just about to leave the room when he called me back. 'So you never did go off to France?' he asked.

I shook my head.

He nodded; up close, his face was sallow, with deep, flute-like grooves. His eyes were submerged beneath a ruck of protuberant lids, while his mouth had suffered a similar regression to the point at which his lips were barely visible. The only consistency in his appearance, though by no means a redeeming feature, was a look of indissoluble gloom.

'I did think, that when you didn't come to ours last Christmas, it was because you were going to stay in France for a while,' he went on. 'I thought you were set on it.'

'Yes well, there was a time when I really wanted to go,' I said. When it came to Uncle Andrew I had never dealt with anything other than apparent indifference; this was new, and I struggled to know how to be. 'I suppose, I mean the idea of being among mountains and everything…I don't know, I just thought it was a bit silly in the end. I mean I guess it looked like I was panicking, after Mum had gone, you know. And after…Benny…'

'That wasn't your fault. And it was over two years ago, now. You have to move on.' Uncle Andrew had never said as much before.

'I still feel like it was my fault. His parents would agree. If I'd just gone home with him after that stupid row we had. If I hadn't insisted on walking, on clearing my head – what a pathetic turn of phrase that is – then he'd never have gone down that road, looking for me. He'd never have wound up…'

'Well, listen, we should have been there for you, more. I'm embarrassed, Jo. Whatever your Grandmother said about it that day, she didn't mean it. She doesn't always mean what she says.'

'When it comes to me, she absolutely does. She wanted a Leah for a granddaughter, and she got a Jo. I often think you all wanted a Leah, maybe another Wendy. Not this. Not a Jo.'

'I was thinking about something over dinner,' he said. He pointed a finger at the window, I thought to indicate something in the distance, but his discourse suggested he was retracing old memories. 'We used to walk through Mason's Forest, my parents and your mum and I. Father would always walk a few paces ahead. And in the evenings, after work, he…I mean he really wasn't at home an awful lot. He was a very good man, Jo, but…' He took a sip of gin from his glass, and continued:

'We'd always talked about going off to Canada, my pal Frankie and I – you know Frankie, don't you? Works just out of town, got a son a bit younger than you. They were just pipedreams, really. He'd liked Anne Ferris since we were thirteen – I don't know if you ever met her – and we'd always go round to hers for barbeques in the summer. And in the winter – when the winters were crisp – we'd pretend to walk to school and cut down Mason's Lane instead, which brought us out on the far side of the woods by the sledging fields. First sign of snow, we'd hide the sledges in the barn and pick them up on our way. You don't get snow like that these days.

'Anne had these big green eyes, like planets. You know the hardest times were when Frankie would place his hand on her shoulder, and she'd glance in my direction. I suppose, I don't know, I suppose I wanted to…but I had to remain loyal to Frankie, he was a decent bloke. When my mother hung out the clothes to dry, I used to find myself wondering how anyone could just be content with…how anyone could go about their lives without…'

I edged my hand towards his, placed it, and we sat for a time together.

'They were married, in the end,' he went on. 'He told me she was all he ever wanted. And she seemed, well, very happy, I suppose. So I took steps to remain a good friend: cycling on a Monday, darts on a Friday, and never quite meeting her eye…'

He paused to draw breath, swallowed and cast his eyes downwards, before resuming his vacant gaze out of the window.

'So that was that, Jo. That really was that. I suppose what I'm trying to say is, well, is that I always admired how your life was like an arrow, how you made a plan and followed it through. I mean you never did what someone said you should

*The Tammersford Lot*

do. *Should* has played all too big a part in my life. My choices were buried in that snow. My, how those winters were cold.'

'Dad.' Colum was just outside the door, his face illuminated, his large frame hidden by the shadows in the hallway.

'Time to make a move, do you think?' asked Uncle Andrew, straightening up.

'Craig's ready to go. He asked if I'd carry Leah to the car - she's fast asleep.'

Uncle Andrew forced the window closed and cleared his throat. I was suddenly struck by the realisation that I'd never made my announcement, and moved about on the spot, one foot to the other and back. My nerves were at once taut; I heard Aunty Wendy and Craig waking Grandmother. Reason told me I ought to do away with my plans; but surely such a linear and time-consuming thought process with an outcome as logical as this had to be validated?

'I'm going to live in Holland for a while,' I half whispered. Colum and Uncle Andrew turned to look at me, seemingly taken aback. 'I'm going to paint the tulips, you know, and just get away for a while, maybe meet someone. I'm not sure when I'll return.'

'Well,' said Uncle Andrew. 'I mean, how will you get there?'

'Well nothing's set in stone yet. I mean, it's just an idea actually, a childish whim, nothing booked or anything, it's...' I tailed off, feeling suddenly ashamed; to divert attention, I began gathering together everyone's coats. 'It's really just an idea I came up with - nothing to get worked up about at this stage. I suppose I'll see you all soon, anyway. Thanks ever so much for coming, it's been great to catch up.'

'Yes, thanks for all your efforts, Jo,' said Aunty Wendy, following Grandmother and Craig into the hallway. 'You'll have to come to us next.'

'Thanks, yes, that would be lovely.'

I told Grandmother to mind her step. From Craig, a pair of parting syllables for my sins: 'Cheers, Cus.' Uncle Andrew hovered, Colum in tow.

'Don't mention it, you'll wake Leah.' I added, 'Really, it was just a whim. Let's not make anything of it, I mean really, I don't think I'll be going. Thank you for coming. This was…nice.'

It was Uncle Andrew who closed the door. His goodbye was constitutive of a nod, a short roster of customary phrases. I went to the kitchen window. The rain beat against the glass, hard, and my family's image was watery and indistinct. Thoughts went immediately to Colum walking alone in the rain, and nodding in complaisance at work; then they turned to Uncle Andrew on the sledging fields, looking at anything but Anne. I wanted to wrench the window open and call down 'I won't go, really, I'm not going to go!' I wanted to tell them that I barely had a handle on the Dutch tenses. I placed my hands on the window. But despite the scrim of rain, Grandmother's sudden gestures were unmistakeable; a fluttering of hands as Colum lowered Leah into the car as if to say, 'mind her head, mind her head!' And from nowhere, or rather deeply, unfathomably somewhere, I felt my heart squeezed to nothing, reduced to the sinewy tufts that held its shape; tough as a cheap cut; dry as the pithy innards of a fallen rowan berry. Instead, I pressed my forehead against the glass and let my eyes follow the car until it drove out of sight.

The house was quiet. On account of a returning ache for self-completion, the logical thing to do, the only thing to do at this stage, was to reach for my grammar notes. I scanned them for twenty of what I considered to be the most commonly-used verbs and began to make a future-tense construction for each of them, adding the odd negative clause and varying the subject now and again. That way, among the tulips and the evening strolls and the occasional downpour, I wouldn't be talking about myself the whole time.

## **Anne Moon**

By all accounts, it was Christmas time. The lights, green and red, blue in places, said as much. Anne could see Christmases past even now, because they were reprised, each of them, in the colourful illuminations that bewebbed the whole town. There, in the middle of things, the tree; a gaudy affair, she thought, too high and mighty for Tammersford.

Tammersford. The name barely meant anything since they had moved away. Standing on the platform of Tammersford train station, shopping bags in hand, a tad lopsided, she concluded, as she did after each visit, that it had become a chore. A place to go when things needed doing. There was a hospital, where dying people went; a church, for marriages and funerals; shops, for your bits and pieces. Really, it was just a necessary evil. That was a fine term, she thought. Something her son would say. Above her, stars pricked tatters of cloud.

That morning, she had rubbed cream into her skin – arms and legs, the lot – brushed her fringe, and checked her breasts. She had thought, it won't rain today, and besides, days indoors, with strange central heating headaches, had conspired to bring her out. It mightn't be all that bad, she thought. But, worse for her, she struggled to pull bad apart, to convey that medley of unpleasant feelings that returned every time she came back here. And then who would understand? Her son, yes, but the stoicism of motherhood – at least the version she'd picked up – precluded that conversation. Her husband?

'We are sorry to announce that the seventeen – thirty – five train to…'

'Oh, for goodness' sake-'

'…has been delayed by approximately twelve minutes.'

'For goodness' sake.'

Underfoot, for the first time in two years, the shallower puddles had iced over. What if snow were to fall, heavily, all at once, white as a wedding? Anne thought back to the last time she was here, in Tammersford. That wedding had been all but rained off. What if she brought out her old snow boots and took a sledge up Mason's Lane? She could hear her husband now:

'Sledging? Bit old for that caper, aren't you? Don't be so bloody daft, woman.'

Or thereabouts.

How on earth would she explain, in that case, that she was late home that evening because her feet, quite of their own accord, had suddenly decided to march her back through the town, through the square, past the old bandstand, the crowds, and up towards the moorland and Mason's Forest? The air was achingly cold as she walked. How would she tell him – her husband of nearly thirty years – that she'd wandered almost to the top of Mason's Lane, where it was slightly warmer, she noticed, but only the way a church feels when you come in from the cold, before you realise that you can still see your breath. How would she tell him that she had seated herself on a stone wall and gazed down at Tammersford for the best part of an hour? She half expected old feelings to surface from somewhere in girlhood, but, as is generally the way of things, they surely wouldn't come now that she'd thought about them, the way dreams don't come if you plan them through. That was in spite of the all the twinkly lights: red, green, blue, and yellow, now, when she looked down on the town in its entirety.

'Snow.'

A wasted imperative. Her son would like it up here, and he'd not make any bones about having to explain himself. Perhaps that was the thing about the young, Anne thought. Candid. But then they'd never know crisp winters.

'Go on, snow. Just for once. I dare you.'

The reply was couched in still and cold terms. Between her and the lights, the forest; modest now, what with the trees being dead, and a good portion of them felled at the forest's edge.

Above, there was a gap in the clouds, and stars looked down, concerned.

'Oh, don't you be worrying about me,' Anne told them. 'I'll manage. Have done for thirty years.'

Likely she wouldn't explain, when she got home, that is, that she had looked at the stars some time, and made patterns out of them. A bin, a corset, turtles. A girl, thirteen, wading through snow, looking this way, looking that, Andy and Frank, liking them both, in the way thirteen year olds do. What she couldn't see was the girl – woman, you might say, at a push – in Tammersford church, all in white, looking only forwards as she suddenly learned the way of things, the way you don't ask, don't tell, the way you turn a blind eye, hastily, if you walk in on your mother, naked, in the bathroom, as though you never noticed her one breast, and the scar, a small, silver-white star anise, binding skin to skin. Likely she wouldn't tell her son that, really, she admired how he brought his thoughts to the fore, unfiltered, intact.

Likely she'd just squeeze his hand when she got home. Below, Tammersford glinted, altogether a shy town, perhaps, a victim; Anne thought, it wasn't its fault. Likely, he might repeal his hand for a moment, like a spider sensing something in its remit, before relaxing into her grasp. Then he might nod, knowing what she meant anyway, knowing more than she'd perhaps ever given him credit for, but he'd play along for her sake, tactfully saving his spirit for more vehement challengers.

She looked to the skies (how strange that the clouds had all but disappeared, now) and willed the stars to have him, her husband, turn a blind eye for an evening. In her own time, she would call off the search for Anne Moon, straighten her fringe, and – bags in hand, taking care not to slip – make her way home. So she began her prayer, tentatively, but in earnest. Eyes closed, the drop on her cheek could have been anything, but in her mind's eye, it was the first snow.

Thank-you for buying and reading

# The Tammersford Lot

We hope you enjoyed it.

If so,
We would be honoured if you leave a review on the Facebook page

**www.facebook.com/Tammersford**

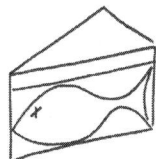

***Fishcake Publications***

The Independent Publisher with the Author in Mind

Other Books are available from Fishcake Publications
See our website and our webstore at
**www.fishcakepublications.com**
for information on where to find them.

The following pages are some of latest releases available as paperback and eBook…

# A Fistful of Marigolds by Joyce Worsfold

It's the beginning of new school term in 1973 and Kathy Johnson needs a fresh start.

Thirty, unmarried and an overworked teacher in a primary school on a run-down council estate, she is beginning to feel that life has passed her by. She needs to move on, but is still haunted by a tragic secret from her past.

However, the disadvantaged people of Becklefield have problems of their own and it's not long before Kathy is irresistibly, compassionately and sometimes unwillingly drawn into their tumultuous lives. A devastating fire; mice and marigolds, parental abuse and apathy, community poverty and passion, plus knights, castles, cub scouts and hilarious days out to the seaside all become entwined into yet another hectic school year. Kathy needs faith and hope to get through and perhaps with the help of the loving church community she can.

Add to that a boy obsessed by Beethoven, a girl who finds hope through a love of flowers and the confusion of several children from the estate all sharing one father exquisitely wrapped up in two poignant love stories, one delightfully her own, and the heart-warming tale of Kathy's life turns prejudices and assumptions upside down and tells just *how it is* in the chaotic neighbourhood surrounding an inner-city primary school.

# Murgatroyd's Christmas Club by Steven Bailey

Skint! Broke! Pennyless! Hard-up!

Willie Arkenthwaite, an ignorant, rude and terribly crude dyehouse worker in Murgatroyd's Mill is feeling a bit poor after his Christmas break and returns to work a troubled man. Not only does he have to put with the nagging mother-in-law at home, but he has a family (and pigeons) to look after and he fears next Christmas will be just as tight.

Until one day this normally docile and inarticulate man does something he's never done before – he has an idea. Willie wants to start a Christmas savings club.

So what does he know about running a club? Nothing.

What does he know about setting up a committee? Nothing.

Has he ever saved before? Definitely not.

Luckily his best friend, Arthur Baxter, who has visions of grandeur, is a little bit more organised and is able to help Willie along and before he knows it, he's the Treasurer.

What does he know about being a Treasurer? Nothing.

So how on earth will this man be able to collect his wits about him and make next Christmas better for everyone? Well, with the help of his whimsical friends and workmates, a kind and generous mill boss and a eclectic local Yorkshire village community (and not forgetting his tolerant wife), he might just be able to pull it off although you can guarantee, where Willie's concerned, there's bound to be some mishaps on the way.

## Murgatroyd's Mill Trip by Stephen Bailey

Breakfast, bus, beer, Blackpool…bust!

The Christmas club was a great success, the Christmas club social evening passed by with only one incident and Willie, Arthur and Eustace were feeling pretty good about themselves; especially Eustace who, on the back of that one incident, was beginning to have a turnaround in his life.

But has Eustace bitten off more than he can chew when he decides he is going to organise the Murgatroyd mill trip to Blackpool? He thinks not, but then…it is Eustace.

The normally down-trodden, stuttering, bumbling fool that is Eustace is bound to stumble his way through this minefield of potential problems but, as usual, he has his friends Willie and Arthur to back him up. But could that make things worse?
If organising the trip wasn't hard enough, imagine the things that could go wrong with a bus full of drunken mill workers enjoying the delights of sunny Blackpool.

Liaisons with 'ladies' on another trip?

Escaping the clutches of Madame Zsa Zsa?

Kidnapping a donkey?

Crashing the bus?

How is Eustace and his friends going to get out of this series of mishaps? After all, they are responsible and the police are always involved…

## Education! Education! Murder!

A break in, a robbery and a hideous murder at a local primary school.

This is a hideous and unusual event in the dreary mill town of Telbury where Detective Inspector Marcus Harrison finds himself after transferring from the big city against his will. At least now he has a case to get his teeth into that will take his mind off his own troubles.

But is it such a simple case?

Surely these events are related, aren't they?

With such an unpopular victim, suspiciously acting staff, blackmail, corruption and vice all being uncovered, finding the murder may be tricky.

If working through these issues wasn't enough, the discovery of a second body throws all reasoning out of the window.

Only with help from an unexpected source can DI Harrison bring the killer to justice.